DREAM TIME

NEW STORIES BY SIXTEEN AWARD-WINNING AUTHORS

DREAM TIME

Edited by Toss Gascoigne
Jo Goodman, Margot Tyrrell

Illustrated by
Elizabeth Honey

Houghton Mifflin Company
Boston 1991

Library of Congress Cataloging-in-Publication Data

Dream time : new stories by sixteen award-winning authors / edited by
  Toss Gascoigne, Jo Goodman, and Margot Tyrrell : illustrated by
  Elizabeth Honey.
     p. cm.
  Summary: A collection of sixteen short stories, produced by asking
authors recognized or awarded by the Australian Book Council to
write on the theme of "Dream Time."
  ISBN 0-395-57434-X
  1. Children's stories, Australian.   2. Australia—Juvenile
fiction. [1. Australia—Fiction.   2. Short stories.]
I. Gascoigne, Toss.   II. Goodman, Jo.   III. Tyrrell, Margot.
IV. Honey, Elizabeth, ill.
PZ5.D748   1991   90-48590
[Fic]—dc20   CIP
                       AC

Printed in the United States of America

BP   10   9   8   7   6   5   4   3   2   1

CONTENTS

PREFACE

This collection of stories is a tribute to the Australian Children's Book Council. For the last forty years, the Council has recognised the best in Australian children's literature with its Book of the Year Awards. Sixteen authors, whose books have either won or been commended in the Awards since 1976, were invited to write stories especially for this anthology.

The theme the authors were given was 'Dream Time', and they were free to respond to this idea in any way they wished. Their contributions are wonderfully varied and imaginative – some are humorous, some poignant, some mysterious. We liked them all, and we hope you do too.

DOLPHIN DREAMING
Gillian Rubinstein

Lizzie hardly cried at all when her father died. Everyone said it would have been much better if she had. But she was only eight, and it was as though she couldn't grasp what had happened. She seemed to be more puzzled than anything, puzzled and rather angry, as though he had let her down by dying. She started waking at night and wandering into her mother's room and saying in a sharp questioning voice, 'Daddy? Daddy?'

Her mother found this much more unnerving than tears. Lara, who was three years older, cried extravagantly, as she always did everything, and the weeping helped to lessen the dreadful pain of loss. But Lizzie did not cry; instead she became angry and fearful as well as pale and thin.

Once school ended for the summer, none of them could bear the thought of Christmas without Dad.

'I wish we could go to the Peninsula,' Lara said one morning, looking wearily at her cereal. Lizzie was still sleeping, having woken them up several times in the night.

Mum was about to drink a mouthful of tea. Instead she stopped with the cup half-way to her lips, and gazed thoughtfully at Lara. 'That's just what I was thinking last night! Would you really like to? I think it would be so good for us all to get away, but you know how much Dad loved it over there. I'm afraid it will bring back too many memories.'

'Everything here brings back too many memories anyway,' Lara pointed out, blinking hard. 'At least there there'll be a bit more space around them.'

Now she had started thinking about it she was filled with longing, as though the wide sweep of the bay, the white, empty dunes and the turquoise water held some power that would heal her. Perhaps Mum felt the same thing. She put down her tea, gave Lara a grin that was nearly as good as her old ones, and jumped up from the table.

'Come on, Lara. Let's get going. You get the camping list, and get the gear together. I'll organise the food.'

Getting on the road was as exciting as ever, and Lara found that she could almost forget about her father for a little while. When they were away from home his death did not seem so final, more like he had gone on a trip, and would be back in a few days. Her grief lifted, and when they came to the end of the four-hour journey, and the Subaru nosed carefully but firmly onto the white sands of the bay, she gave a hoot of excitement.

They set up camp in the dunes, putting up the tent and the cooking annex, organising the Eskies, the stove and the water bottles. Lara had never realised how much work there was to do, and Mum was looking exhausted by the time it was all finished, especially since Lizzie was being no help at all. She seemed to be getting angrier and angrier, and she shouted at her sister when Lara asked her to hold a rope.

'What's the matter with you?' Lara said. 'You've got to help a little bit, since Dad's not here.'

'Where is he?' Lizzie shouted even louder. 'I thought he was going to be here! I thought that was why we came!' Her face was red and angry, and her eyes were bright, but the tears were tears of rage, and anyway they remained unshed.

'Oh darling,' Mum said. 'Daddy's not here. He's dead. He died in the car accident.'

When they unpacked the swimming gear something caught Lara's eye at the bottom of the bag.

'Look, Mum,' she exclaimed, pulling it out. 'It's Dad's shell necklace!'

It was a short string of white shells that her father had worn on the beach, telling the children it was his last souvenir of the days when he was a surfie. Lara gazed at it sadly. It brought back such strong memories of him, she could almost feel him next to her. It seemed so strange that the necklace should still be there while he was not. It was too precious a thing to put back in the bag, so she put it round her own neck, where it lay cool against the brown skin, just above her collar bones. Then she cried again, and so did Mum, and the unpacking had to be interrupted while they held each other. But Lizzie ran away up the beach and threw stones at rocks.

Finally everything was done. Mum boiled up a kettle of water on the gas stove and made a cup of tea. She and Lara looked proudly at the little camp. They both felt a strong satisfaction, and relief that they had done it on their own. They had taken another step without him. They were sad, but they were going to survive.

'We'll make a fire on the beach later,' Mum said, 'and cook

sausages and beans on it. But why don't we have a swim now, while it's still warm?'

Lara and Lizzie ran down to the water with their face masks and snorkels. Lara dived straight in, but when she surfaced through the clear, sparkling water, Lizzie was still standing on the edge.

Mum came up to her and took her hand gently. 'Come on, darling, we'll go in together.' But Lizzie twisted away.

'I don't want to go in! There are too many crabs!'

When she was little she had been terrified of crabs. Dad used to carry her into the sea so she did not have to put her feet on the sand. Last summer she had walked in through the wavelets fearlessly. Now, however, the crabs seemed to have returned.

'Don't be such a sook, Lizzie,' Lara called meanly. She was afraid Lizzie was going to spoil the holiday, and she hated seeing the sad, worried look that came into Mum's eyes every time Lizzie got difficult.

'Just stay on the edge, then,' Mum said. 'I must get in the water or I'll die!'

She and Lara swam together, following shoals of fish, across the clean, smooth sand into enchanted worlds of rocks and seaweed. When they looked up to check on Lizzie she was by the high water mark, strolling along, head down, eyes on the ground, stopping every few steps to crouch down and examine something on the beach.

'She's a strandlooper,' Lara said, hoping to see Mum smile. It was their father's word, one that he had gleaned from some book or other and handed on to them: *strandlooper*, the strange ancient race that once lived on the South African coast and loved beautiful shells.

Mum did smile. 'I hope she's finding some treasures to cheer her up.'

When they came out of the water and ran back to the

camp to wrap themselves in their towels, Lizzie had arranged her treasures in a little hollow in the dunes. Around the edge was a circle of pipi shells, bleached white and mauve streaked, broken up every now and then by a shiny grey oyster with craggy white edges. In the middle was a most unusual bone, like a cross or a four-pointed star. There were lines radiating out from the centre almost as though it had been carved, and when Lara picked it up to look at it more closely she could see that there were holes in it, as though it had once hung on a string around someone's neck.

'What is it, Mum?'

Mum took it from her. 'I think it's some sort of vertebra – part of the backbone.' She ran her hand down the knobbles on Lara's spine. 'But I don't know what sort of animal it's from.' She put it back carefully in the centre of the circle. 'It's lovely, Lizzie. You were clever to find such a treasure!'

Lizzie smiled a little then. 'It's mine,' she said proudly. 'I found it!'

'You are a clever little strandlooper,' Lara told her. 'Let's all go strandlooping after dinner, Mum. I bet I can find some treasures too!'

Mum found an old green bottle, and Lara found a little brown glass jar which they were thrilled with, and Lizzie found some more treasures to add to her collection: a sea-urchin shell, unhusked by the sea, and a piece of driftwood that looked like a goanna. By the time they got back to the tent it was nearly dark. Mum lit the gas lamps and built up the fire. Lara made hot chocolate with marshmallows, and she and Mum sang 'Botany Bay' and 'The Lime Juice Tub', 'The North Wind' and 'The Colours of Christmas', but their voices sounded thin and high without Dad's deeper voice beneath them, and after a few songs everyone decided to go to sleep, rather than sit up with their memories under the stars.

All the same, Lara did not feel unhappy as she snuggled down inside her sleeping bag and in the night Lizzie only woke once to say 'Daddy!'

Magpies woke Lara next morning, long before the sun was up over the land. She crawled out of the tent and went to look for her mother whom she found a little way inland, among the dunes, under a small tree. Two magpies were sitting above her, and from where Lara stood they looked as if they were talking to each other.

'What did the magpies say to you?' she asked curiously as the two of them walked back to the tent together.

Mum laughed. She had her country face on, quite different from her city one, and she looked as though someone had been sweeping out her spirit overnight. 'It's funny,' she said, 'but I just love magpies. I feel as though they are my sisters. And, do you know, I have never, ever been attacked by one.'

'If you were a Nungga they would be your totem,' Lara said. She had learned about this at school.

'That's exactly what I think,' Mum replied. 'And when we are out here the land speaks to me so clearly, I could sit and listen to it forever.'

Lara stopped and listened to the land. She could feel it stretching and changing as the sun warmed it. She could hear its myriad animal and plant voices, underpinned by the constant murmur of the sea, and by something else that spoke directly to her own spirit, that told her she was its child.

'Oh, I can hear it too,' she cried, and she and Mum hugged each other.

Lizzie had come out to see where they were, and was staring at them almost jealously.

'Someone else is here!' she announced.

'Here?' Mum repeated in surprise, but what Lizzie meant was another family had set up camp in the night about 500 metres along the beach. A four-wheel drive vehicle was parked on the sand, with two bright coloured tents already erected behind it, and a trailer with a boat and outboard engine alongside it.

'I don't like them,' Lizzie said crossly. 'This is our own private place.'

Lara felt the same, but Mum sighed and said, 'They've got as much right to be here as we have.'

Later they were glad the other camp was there, for none of them was able to open the bottle of gherkins to have with lunch. Lara and Lizzie walked along the beach with the bottle, and the father of the family took it in his brown, strong hands and turned the lid as easily as turning on a tap.

'There you go, love,' he said to Lara, handing the bottle back to her. 'No worries. You like fish? You come up in the morning, I'll have some fresh snapper or whiting, with luck.'

There were two boys, Chris, who looked about the same age as Lara, and Alex who was a little bit younger than Lizzie. They both had black hair and golden brown skin and they wore brightly coloured board shorts. Chris was so thin his board shorts were in danger of falling down altogether, but Alex had a little roll of puppy fat above his, and his legs were chubby. They were very friendly and after giving the girls a can of coke and showing them their camp and their boat, they walked back with them to say hello to Mum.

Later the children swam together; at least, Chris and Lara swam while Alex jumped up and down on the edge, and Lizzie stayed far up by the high water mark.

'Come in, Alex!' his brother called to him, but the little boy shook his head, and when Chris went back to lead him in, Alex cried and struggled.

'He's frightened of the sea,' Chris explained to Lara. 'He thinks there are sharks.'

'My sister thinks there are crabs!' Lara said, and then she wanted to stand up for Lizzie, so she added, 'But it's only because she's little.'

'I was never frightened of sharks or crabs even when I was little,' Chris said rather disgustedly. 'Alex is a sook about everything! He's a dead loss!'

By the end of the day Lara agreed thoroughly with this remark and she had almost decided Lizzie was a dead loss too. Alex cried about everything, and Lizzie got in rages. Finally Lara and Chris left them to it, and ran down to have an evening swim when the tide was at its fullest.

After the blazing day the sun was setting into a purple sea and turning the sky the colour of rock-melon. The water where they swam was dark, almost purple too, paling to green above the reef.

'Look!' Chris exclaimed, seizing Lara's arm. 'Dolphins!'

She gazed entranced as the sleek black bodies surfaced through the water. They were close enough for the children to see their clever, merry eyes and their hard grey beaks.

The magic of the moment was broken by screams from the shore. Lara and Chris stared in astonishment as Alex came running through the dunes, pursued by a furious Lizzie. Mum appeared from behind the tent, and captured Lizzie as she dashed by. Alex went on running doggedly towards his own tent, and as he ran he scattered something behind him.

'Oh no!' Lara said. 'I think he's got her treasures!' Taking a last reluctant look at the dolphins she galloped out of the water, and Chris followed her.

Lizzie was shrieking hysterically in Mum's arms. 'He stole my things!' she yelled. 'I showed him my treasures and he ran away with them.'

'I'll get them back,' Chris promised. 'Don't cry, I'll make him give them back.'

But Alex had scattered the treasures all over the sand, and though they found the driftwood goanna and the sea-urchin shell, and a lot of shells that might have been Lizzie's, search as they might they could not find the strange bone.

'It was my favourite,' Lizzie said forlornly. 'It was the best treasure I ever found.'

Chris made Alex come back and say he was sorry, and Mum got out lemonade and chips for everyone while she boiled up the water for spaghetti. The dolphins came back and swam up and down through the darkening sea, but even they did not cheer Lizzie up.

Lara went to see if she could help Mum, and found her staring at the sea while the water bubbled and boiled onto the gas stove.

'I was looking at the dolphins,' Mum said, rescuing the spaghetti. 'And remembering how much Dad loved them. Sometimes I feel as if he's just gone for a walk down the beach, and when he comes back I can tell him about them.'

In the middle of the night Lara woke up. The moon was bright on her face through the tent door, and the sleeping bag next to her was empty. She struggled out of her own bag, hot and thirsty, and went to get a drink of water from the ice-box. As she was drinking, she saw a shadowy shape on the beach, half-way between the dunes and the sea.

'Lizzie?' she whispered, going towards it. It was Lizzie. She was walking to and fro, her eyes fixed on the sand.

'What are you doing out of bed?' Lara said gently, taking hold of her arm carefully, in case she was sleepwalking. But Lizzie was wide awake. 'I'm looking for my bone,' she said in a normal voice, making Lara jump. 'I woke up and I couldn't get back to sleep and I thought I'd be able to find it 'cause the moon's so bright.'

'I'll look too,' Lara said. The beach at night was beautifully mysterious, with black shadows on the white sand, and the brilliant moon above. The waves hissed gently on the shore, and the endless sea stretched away into the night. Out towards the horizon little lights showed where people were fishing from boats. Chris and his dad were probably out there somewhere, Lara thought, and she wondered if the dolphins were there, too.

They searched the sand for a long time but they could not find the bone. Lara wanted to give up, but Lizzie grew more stubborn. Finally Lara suggested, more in desperation than anything else, 'Let's sit down for a bit and listen to the spirit of the land. Perhaps it'll tell us where the bone went to.'

Perhaps Lizzie was tired too; anyway, to Lara's relief she sat down rather grumpily on the dry sand above the high water mark. Lara sat down next to her. 'Put your head on my shoulder and close your eyes,' she said.

After a few moments Lizzie said sleepily, 'I can't hear anything,' and yawned.

'Listen a bit harder,' Lara said, her eyes closed too, and then they suddenly both heard something at the same time, and they opened their eyes with a start.

Out in the sea, something was splashing. They could see the white spray against the black water.

'It must be the dolphins,' Lara said softly. 'Look, Lizzie, aren't they magic!'

The dark shapes glistened as they caught the moonlight. They were coming closer and closer to the shore.

Lizzie said incredulously, 'They're carrying something!'

Between them the dolphins were shouldering a fragile, helpless burden, a figure that floated in the water, limbs trailing. The dolphins held up its head with their strong beaks and nudged it through the shallows until it lay on the sand, nose and mouth free of water, able to breathe air again.

'It's a man!' Lara exclaimed, and made to get up, but at that moment the scene faded, and they could see nothing. At first Lara thought the moon had gone behind a cloud but then she remembered that the night was cloudless and she realised that they were seeing something that happened a long, long time ago.

When the darkness cleared and they could see again the man was standing upright on the beach, facing out to sea. He was a wonderful looking man, like a god or a hero, Lara said later to her mother, with rippling, shining black skin, and thick, black hair that curled around his head and glistened under the moon like the dolphins. When he turned to face the land, the children could see his broad noble nose and his huge, dark, deepset eyes. His body was painted with glowing white marks and he wore decorations of shells around his neck and limbs.

As they watched he began to dance. He danced swimming far out at sea, and then he danced himself drowning and the dolphins rescuing him. He danced the dolphins bringing him into land, so accurately that the girls had to blink their eyes once or twice to check they were not seeing a dolphin dancing a man. Then the man raced towards the water and dived into the sea and the dolphins came and danced with him in the shallows until darkness fell again.

Lizzie shivered and Lara sighed deeply, but neither girl could move away. They peered expectantly through the dark, waiting to see what happened next.

When they could see again they both cried out. A dolphin lay stranded on the beach, and the man sat on his heels next to it, wailing with grief.

'Oh, the poor dolphin!' Lara wailed, and Lizzie said urgently, 'What's happened to it? What's happened to it?'

'The dolphin is dead!' Lara said, and next to her Lizzie sobbed quietly, 'The dolphin is dead!'

Then they both hid their faces and cried fresh tears like springwater, and when they looked again the man was sitting a few metres away from them, singing a low chant and holding something in his hand, something that hung around his neck on a string.

'Don't be afraid,' Lara whispered to Lizzie. 'I don't think he can see us.'

'I'm not afraid of him,' Lizzie replied simply. 'He's a dolphin man, and look, he's wearing my bone!'

Still chanting the dolphin man rose and, stooping low, drew in the clean, sea-washed sand. He drew the shape of a dolphin, and then he took the bone from his neck and placed it at a certain point in its tail. Then he sang a high-pitched, clicking song, and danced his dolphin dance around the bone.

A splash in the shallows told the children the dolphins were there, watching.

Everything faded, and when the moon returned Lizzie's bone lay a few metres away from them in the sand.

'There it is!' Lara said in surprise. 'However did we miss it before?'

'The dolphin man brought it back,' Lizzie said sleepily. She picked it up, and as they staggered off to the tent and their sleeping bags she was clutching it firmly in her hand.

'Do you think it was a dream?' Lara asked Mum the next morning.

Mum smiled at her. There were tears in her eyes, but they were not really sad ones.

'You can cry, Mum!' Lizzie said generously, giving her a tissue. 'But don't worry about Dad. He's like the dolphin man. He's dead, but he's still somewhere. Here, or somewhere else. Let's go swimming now.'

'Here come Alex and Chris,' Lara said. 'I expect they've brought us some fish.'

'You can come swimming with me, Alex,' Lizzie announced. 'I won't let anything get you. The dolphins look after me, 'cause I'm a dolphin girl!'

'What about the crabs?' Chris asked, teasingly.

'The crabs are just getting on with living, just like us,' Lizzie said.

*   *   *

For the rest of the holiday they swam and explored the dunes with Chris and Alex, went out in their boat and went strandlooping along the shore. Every day the dolphins in the bay watched them. When it was time to go home, Lizzie grew quieter and quieter as they packed up the camp.

'Are you all right, darling?' Mum asked anxiously. 'I suppose you don't want to leave.'

Lizzie nodded and smiled, but she said nothing until they were in the car, and half-way down the dirt track leading away from the beach. Then she said in a sudden, small voice, 'Mum, do you mind going back?'

'Whatever for?' Mum said in surprise.

'Well, I've got a horrible feeling about taking my bone away. I think it wants to stay here.'

Mum stopped the car, very patiently turned it round, and drove slowly back to their camp site.

'Why does it want to stay here?' Lara questioned.

'This is where it belongs. This is where its dreams happen,' Lizzie replied slowly.

'Where its dreams happen,' Lara repeated to herself. As she followed Lizzie across the sand that was still wet from last night's tide, she undid the clasp of her father's necklace.

They stopped at a point half-way between the dunes and the sea, and Lizzie dug a hole and buried the bone. Then Lara dug a hole a little way from it and buried the necklace.

When they got to their feet, they saw the dolphins leap and dive through the turquoise water.

'Both home now,' Lara said to herself. 'Both dolphin men have come home.'

UP TAREE WAY
Libby Hathorn

The idiots at the back of the hall were quiet once Neil
Symon started speaking. Even the smartarse Leandra Evans
was quiet and Shane Winter forgot to cough like he usually
did when there were talks on. The old man's voice, rich and
deep, was important. It rang through the darkened room and
made everyone feel shivery.

*In the Dreamtime, a long ago, a far off time, there was a big
darkness all over the land. They came, those Ancestral Beings
then, the good spirits. They carved the beautiful land, shaping it this way and that as they went, making the beautiful
animals too – the kangaroo, the possum and the lyrebird . . .*
His hand moved swiftly through the air, making big sweeping
shapes as he talked, as if he was conducting . . . *the goanna,*

the snake and the kookaburra. They left their paths all over this land, the Ancestral Beings. They made the hills and the gullies. They made the rocks and the trees and the rivers . . . and they made the first people in the Dreamtime long ago.

They listened so quietly you could hear a pin drop. There was something magic about that voice.

Milly listened nervously to the words of the old man with the soft brown eyes. Sometimes he spoke as if he was almost singing, she thought. She was glad when he picked up the guitar and he did sing. All the kids clapped along with him then, but she sat still thinking. His voice had somehow worried her. It was good and bad at the same time. It made her remember things. Things she didn't want to remember. It was good – and yet it was full of something deep and painful that she was trying to forget.

'Some old guy Miss Kirby dredged up from the local pub to tell stories. Just so's she can get out of work, I'll bet,' Maureen had said scornfully in the playground. Their English teacher had announced a story session for their class in the hall every morning for a whole week. 'And I s'pose we'll have to answer questions for homework,' she sighed.

'Who is he anyway?' Pete asked.

'Neil Symon, an Aboriginal storyteller,' Nerida said, glancing down at the crumpled notice in her hand. She started reading in Miss Kirby's precise clipped voice. 'He's over 70, boahs and girhls, and he travels round the countrahside telling stories. He's come for a week of stories and workshops at ouah school. And to take part in ouah History Australia Day.'

Pete laughed. 'Sounds okay to me,' but Maureen frowned. 'Hmmm. Well it's going to mean a load more work, I bet.'

'We'll get off some work, you idiot,' Pete insisted, taking the notice from Nerida. 'See there's the History Day on Friday. Miss Kirby says we're having a sausage sizzle and dances and things.'

'I s'pose they'll ask my dad to donate the sausages again,' Nerida said darkly.

'And if there's one thing I hate,' Maureen said, 'it's sausages!'

'Neil Symon. Sounds like a singer or something,' Pete said, and then, 'Hey Milly, he's got the same name as you. Look – Symon spelt the same way. With the "y".'

Milly's stomach clenched into a tight knot. 'So what?' she asked.

'Just thought he might be a relation or something,' Pete said.

Maureen was incensed. 'But Milly's Italian, not *Aboriginal*, you dag.'

Mum had told her not to say that they were Aboriginal and not to say they came from up Taree way. 'Don't say anything about Taree or Forster Beach or Seal Rocks or anything unless they ask,' she'd said in such a worried voice. Milly didn't know who *they* were that her mother feared so much. Maureen, Nerida and Pete, her best friends at Coogee High School maybe?

'You've been to Brisbane once,' Mum said, 'so say you came from there and your dad is Italian. That's if anyone asks. And don't say anything to Bob.'

Bob was Mum's boyfriend. Maureen had seen Mum with him in a pale green sporty-looking car once. 'Gees, your Mum's boyfriend's a spunk, isn't he?'

Milly didn't say she didn't like Bob much at all. Bob hardly spoke to her when he came to their flat. And she didn't like to speak to him in case she said something Mum had told her not to. And she hated the long evenings by herself when they went out.

She was glad Pete lived in the red brick block right next door, or some nights she might go mad with the loneliness.

Pete wasn't a spunk but he was a good friend. Sometimes they did homework together. She liked helping him with English and Maths. Pete wasn't all that good at schoolwork but he was funny and friendly. She never worried too much about what she said to Pete. But like Mum had said, she didn't ever tell their secret. Not to anyone. It seemed important to Mum.

But now, out of the blue, Neil Symon had turned up and she felt all mixed up. She lay awake wondering again, 'Who am I? Who am I not allowed to be? Milly Symon from up Taree way? Not from Brisbane with an Italian father?'

For years now since she was a little girl and they'd left Grandma Pearl and old Bill and all of them up north and come to live in the city by themselves, she'd wondered about herself like this. She'd had a burning dreadful secret and quite often if Mum went on about it, it turned into a burning pain inside her.

'Where did you say your school was when you were little?' Nerida had asked one day when the new boy arrived from Brisbane.

The terrible secret again. She swallowed, 'In Brisbane.'

'Banana land, eh?' Pete had said.

'Well, this is Glen and he's from Brisbane too,' Nerida had said.

'Whereabouts did you live?' Glen asked.

Mum had drilled her well. 'Uh, Holland Park,' she said.

'Hey, what about that place you used to go with your uncle? Round the headland with the cave and the secret rock pool? Glen might know that place,' Pete said enthusiastically.

They had all heard Milly's stories about the beaches she had loved as a little girl. And the adventures she had had with her cousins there.

'No beaches in Brisbane but,' Glen said in a puzzled way. 'None near Holland Park, that's for sure. Must've been down the coast?'

18

'Yeah,' Milly said uneasily, 'it was down the coast where we went on holidays and things.' She fell silent then.

Down, down the coast to Taree, the lovely country town. And then further on to the beautiful beaches, all the way along to the splendid Seal Rocks where she had lived for a while as a very young child. Near the cool beaches and the green forests. Not in hot old Brisbane.

'Hey Milly, tell Glen your cave story. Boy, is it spooky!'

The kids liked listening to Milly's stories. The real ones and the ones she liked to make up. Even the ones she wrote for Miss Kirby.

'Milly's writing a soapie, you know, and she'll send it into Channel 5. It's better than Dynasty, no kidding.'

But Milly didn't want to talk to Glen anymore.

'I'm going to the canteen,' she said, even though the burning feeling in her stomach meant she wouldn't be able to eat.

'There's a note from school,' Milly said. She never bothered Mum with notes usually. Mum was always so tired. But this one, about the Aboriginal storyteller called Neil Symon, spelt with a 'y', she wanted to show her.

'Oh?' Mum dried her hands on the old apron behind the door, the one she never wore. She took the note from Milly and held it at a distance because Mum needed glasses now to read any small print. Milly shot into the lounge room and switched on the TV. She was going to hurt her mother with that note. She was sure of it.

A replay of *The Addams Family* was on and she hunched up in her chair, hardly watching. She was kind of listening to the sprinkles of canned laughter from the TV and the silence from the kitchen.

It wasn't till dinner that Milly said to Mum, 'You read the note from school?'

'Yes,' Mum said, 'about the storytelling and all.' She sounded bored. 'Seems okay.'

'Aboriginal stories, Mum.' She looked up. 'And the storyteller who's come to our school for the whole week – well, his name's Symon. Neil Symon. Spelt the same way as ours. Maybe you know him?'

'Never heard of him,' Mum said, but something in the way she said it, so sharply and loudly, gave her away. Mum attacked her chop then as if she was angry.

She knew Neil Symon all right, Milly was sure of it.

'I know you know him,' she wanted to call out at her mother, but all she said was, 'He's nice.'

'Mmmm.'

'Will you come to the History Day on Friday? Anyone can come. He's telling stories at two o'clock. There's going to be a barbeque.' She knew Mum finished early on Fridays.

'No,' Mum said, 'I can't. I don't have the time. It's a real busy time at work. Belle's going to be away and I'm doing an extra shift this week.' Her voice was loud. 'I just can't come, Milly.'

'Okay. Okay. Don't go on, Mum. I just asked. That's all.' Milly didn't stay at the table and talk to Mum. She went straight to her bedroom.

That night as she lay in her bed wide awake, she thought about Neil's Dreamtime story.

I am the land and the land goes on and on, he had said. She could see the great formless expanse, humped and carved and pressed and pushed into shapes of canyons and gullies and caves and creek-beds and mountains and beaches by the Ancestor Spirits. Even the land under her suburb here at Coogee. Not that you could see much of the land with all the shops and houses. Only at the edge where cliffs and beaches met the sea.

But you could see it and smell it, she remembered suddenly and vividly, in the timber forests or the secret caves or the deep gushing rock pools where she had once lived. And in the strange shaped mountains near home that the highway wove through. She remembered the highway through the mountains, that took them away from everybody she knew and loved. 'It's going to be much better for us in the city where we're going,' Mum had said over and over. But Mum had cried too, when they left.

Some of that countryside they'd left behind was just like it must have been in Neil's Dreamtime, Milly thought with a start. In *her* Dreamtime. But Neil's Dreamtime had turned into her nightmare. She wanted to ask Neil about Taree and Seal Rocks. About Grandma Pearl and Bill. He must know them. She wanted to tell Neil about Mum and herself but she couldn't. When Neil had spoken again today, her heart had spurted with pain just like it had when their little cat had gone. Only difference was she felt as if something she'd lost had been found. But she couldn't have it anyway.

Next day at the story session the kids really liked the way Neil let them act out the stories he told. They laughed like anything when he made Leandra the crow and Shane the dingo in one of the stories about a chase across the land. Shane had been chasing Leandra the whole year.

'He could go on the telly, you know, that old guy,' Pete said. 'He's pretty good.'

'Yeah, he's not as bad as I thought,' Nerida yawned on the third morning.

'And so far no homework from Kirby,' Maureen enthused. 'Hey, didn't Shane look funny though when he jumped into the waterhole? Gees I laughed.'

But on the fourth morning of Neil's stories, when he mentioned some names of places that Milly found she remembered, her heart froze again. The secret cave around from Blackhead Beach, the rainforest near Buledelah Mountain. Purfleet out of Taree where they had friends. And Seal Rocks. He described places that she'd been to – oh, so long ago – when she was little. And now in his magic sing-song voice he

21

told about those places. And she could remember them all, clear as day.

Oh, it was awful. She shouldn't remember this stuff. Mum'd be so mad about it. She felt the burning feeling again in her stomach and in her chest. But she did remember it all now. So clearly too.

A great blue expanse of sea. Humped rocks gouging out into the blueness. Kids on their surfboards taking the waves at the corner. An old weatherboard house and Grandma Pearl taking her hand. Tumbling down onto the beach to pick up shells or to swim at the edge where the frothy lace of foam drenched you. Running back to take Pearl's hand, to show Bill the treasure shells.

'Oh yes, Neil Symon, I know you. I know you,' she rejoiced 'and I know the places that you know – the place you come from. It's my place as well as yours. And I know it.'

'Mum, Neil Symon says he lives near Seal Rocks.'

'So?' Mum said tersely. She was tired. They were both sitting in front of the TV but Milly's thoughts were not on *Young Talent Time*. Her head was full of Neil's stories.

'So . . .' Milly's stomach had the old familiar burning sensation, 'so you might know him, Mum. That's all. I thought he looked a bit, well, a bit familiar. And I thought he might know Grandma, you know, with his name being Symon and all . . .'

Mum turned to her, her eyes blazing. 'I said I don't know him! I wish you'd stop harping on about it. I told you, Milly, to forget all that. Forget those places. That's the past, Milly. It's dead. We live here now. We're new people now.'

'We're the same,' Milly said stubbornly. 'I reckon I am anyway.'

Her mother jumped to her feet, 'What is this, Milly? Do you want to spoil everything for us. Is that it? I told you to forget the past. Now I don't want to hear another word about Neil Symon or Seal Rocks or anything else.'

Mum walked away from her in angry clipping footsteps across the room.

Milly felt tears of anger in her eyes. What was Mum so frightened of? Who were the *they* who would spoil everything for them? And how? It must be Mum's boyfriend, Bob, and his friends. Mum was frightened of Bob knowing. But Bob loves Mum, that's easy to see, and if he really cares, then . . .

Milly lay in the dark that night staring out through the slice of window that the blind did not cover. The old question tormented her. 'Who am I?' she asked herself again and again. 'Who is it that I'm not allowed to be?' She tossed in her bed hot and uncomfortable. She'd upset Mum now and she was angry with herself.

'Well I'm not going to let it get to me. I'll forget it. Like Mum says, I'll forget the past. Why should I worry? I won't think about it anymore. And I won't go to any more of Neil's stories. I won't think about him or them anymore. I won't remember Grandma Pearl and Bill and . . .' She breathed deeply, closing her eyes, willing Neil's voice away. It was peaceful and quiet for a moment.

And then, *I am the land and the land goes on and on* . . . It seemed to be inside the room, inside her head.

She sat up suddenly, angrily, and said out loud, 'All right, Neil Symon, you win! I'm Milly Symon from up Taree way and I bet you're our family. Tomorrow I'm going to ask you. I am! I'm asking about Grandma Pearl and Bill from Seal Rocks and all of the others too. And tomorrow I'm going to tell the kids at school that I'm Milly Symon from up Taree way.' She felt glad when she said this but when she lay back she thought of Mum's angry blazing eyes. Please, Mum, don't be angry with me. Don't get that hard, cold closed-up look you get every time we talk about this. But I've got to know.

The alarm buzzed in her ear. It was Mum's early shift and she'd already gone. Milly pulled up the blind and waved across the side alley of the flats where she could see Pete at his window. He always made faces and mouthed goodmorning to her through the glass. She pushed up the window this morning and motioned him to do the same, 'Pete,' she called across the dampish space between them. 'I reckon that Neil Symon man, you know the storyteller, *is* related to us,' she called. 'I'm going to ask him today.'

'Yeah?' Pete was yawning, 'You do that. Hey Milly, did you do your Maths homework?'

'Yeah, did you?'

'W-e-ell. I went to footy training and then I watched that late movie and Bovis is still down on me about the test.' He yawned again.

'I'll give you mine,' she said. 'You can copy it at the bus stop.'

At school before the story session in the library she told the others that Neil Symon might be her uncle. Nerida said, 'Just because you like telling stories and acting and things and his name's the same spelling ... you're getting a bit carried away, aren't you?'

'Anyway he's Abo!' Maureen said.

'So?' Milly said.

'Well that means that you'd have to be.'

'I guess it does,' Milly said quietly, with her heart thumping.

'So?' Pete said.

'Gees,' was all Maureen said and looked away.

They went into the big auditorium for the concert. There was a bush dance display and the band played folksongs, and then a hush went over the crowd as Neil Symon took the middle of the stage.

'You kids want to know how the sun got in the sky?' he asked.

'Yes,' they all called out together.

'Well then I'm gonna tell you.' He took up his guitar and strummed. He half-sang, half-told the amazing story of how

Bralagah the Crane thew an emu egg into the sky where it hit a pile of wood and burst into flames and how a good spirit saw how beautiful the earth was all lit up. And how Gurgurgaga the Kookaburra was chosen by the good spirit to call out each morning so that the sun-fire is lit every day. Then he picked up his guitar and sang a song and the kids clapped, too.

And then when it was finished he put down the guitar and he talked to them again. That was when Milly felt shivery. He told them about the first time *he* had heard the story. It was when he was a small boy away in the middle of the forest.

'We were camping out in the bush – Buledelah way. My father said he reckoned we'd have a visitor that night. Someone we knew and wanted to see very much would come to our campfire that very night. And sure enough, someone did come. My grandfather. We hadn't seen him in months. But he arrived at our camp in the middle of the bush. And late into the night he told the old stories. Just like I'm telling you. And just like his mum and dad told him.'

'You know, it's a funny thing,' the old man continued in a quiet voice that nevertheless seemed to fill the hall, 'but my people are so close to the land and so close to each other, we know things sometimes before they happen. Like my father did at the campfire.'

'I reckon if any of you were coming to visit me in my house up the coast a way, something would kind of tell me you were coming. Like something's telling me right now that someone here today, right here in this hall, is kind of special to me.'

Pete dug Milly in the ribs.

'Sucked in,' Nerida said admiringly.

Neil picked up the guitar and began another song and the spell of his voice was broken.

Milly's heart was beating fast and gladly. So Neil knew that she was here. Knew that Milly Symon, who was part of the big Symon family, had been sitting and listening, so scared and so delighted every day of the week. He knew she was here, just like that. Even without her saying it. She sat in the hall, not watching and not listening to anything else. She was waiting for the end when everyone would go.

'See you outside then,' Pete had said as he and the others trailed outside. Now, now she would walk down towards him where he'd finished talking to the small knot of kids round him. And she would say, 'Here I am, Milly Symon from up Taree way.' And she would ask about Grandma Pearl and Bill and all of them.

But when the kids finally moved away, Neil stared past Milly and right to the back of the hall. He wasn't smiling now. There was such a strange look in his eyes that Milly didn't know if he was sad or glad. But his voice, even though it was a bit chokey, came out very glad. Very, very glad, Milly thought. 'I knew you were coming today,' Neil said. 'I just knew you'd come today.'

Milly turned around in surprise. Who was there that Neil knew so well? Who was it he had just known would come today? And then she saw who it was all right. She gave such a start.

It was her mother. She was sitting alone at the very back row. It looked as if Mum had been crying but she had a kind of soft look on her face when Neil spoke to her.

'Uncle,' Mum said very quietly.

Then Mum got to her feet and slowly walked down the aisle towards the old man as if she was in a bit of a dream.

'Mum,' Milly said anxiously as she reached her seat, 'Mum, I'm here too.' And then Mum had looked at her, not hard and angry and closed up. Not at all. Mum had put out her hand and Milly took it and squeezed it hard.

Then together they walked towards the old man who stood waiting. He put out both his arms to welcome them.

THE DREAMER
John Marsden

When The Dreamer arrived at National Defence Head-quarters she came, not by jet, not by limousine, not by staff car, but on foot. The guards strutted out of the guard-room asking for her pass, wanting to know her business. Behind them, however, came an officer.

'It's all right, stand aside, let her through,' the officer said.

She escorted The Dreamer to Block K, a low grey building at the end of a long plastic path. The interior of the building was surprisingly comfortable: caramel-coloured carpet and soft pastel walls. The Dreamer was offered an armchair and a cup of coffee. She leaned against a wall and refused the coffee.

'Please tell me in detail what you want,' she said. Her voice was soft, and the officer had to lean forward to hear. The words, spoken with an awkward accent, seemed to linger in the air like a last taste of mist. The officer pressed a button on the wall and, a moment later, two small people entered the room.

'These are Lois and Israel,' the officer said. 'They are the astronauts we have chosen.' She paused. 'Do you see any problems with them?'

'No,' The Dreamer answered. 'There will be no problems of that kind.' Her eyes clouded over. She seemed to drift into a trance for a few moments. But when the officer spoke again The Dreamer focused her eyes quickly and listened with care.

'They are quite aware of the dangers,' the officer continued. 'But we need to know if the technical problems can be overcome. Is a heatproof capsule possible? Can oxygen be supplied? Can you get them there quickly? Can they have a viewing window? And radio contact with Earth? Will their eyes be protected?'

At each question The Dreamer nodded. The officer and the two astronauts relaxed. The officer drew a sheaf of papers from her briefcase. 'Then here is the information you asked for,' she said. 'Everything we have about the Sun. And the scientific instruments we hope you will be able to give them.' She nodded Lois and Israel towards the door. 'We will leave you to study the material.'

When the time came The Dreamer was shown to her room. A double bed, covered with a drab brown doona, was the only large piece of furniture. Beside the bed was a table, with a strong electric lamp. A book about the Sun lay on the table. The two astronauts sat in stiff-backed chairs, at the end of the room, facing the wall.

'It is an old building,' the officer explained. 'We considered soundproofing it, but found it would be too expensive. The budget cuts, as you know, have been a catastrophe for us. So we have adopted other measures, cheaper, but just as effective. This corner of the Base has been sealed off, so that there will be no movement outside. Flight paths for aircraft have been changed. The road outside the Base has been closed until tomorrow. And we've checked the building for dripping taps and loose downpipes. We think we can guarantee you an uninterrupted sleep.'

The astronauts, Lois and Israel, watched The Dreamer's face as the officer spoke. They seemed reassured by her slow nods, as she looked around the room.

'Yes, this is satisfactory,' she said. 'If you leave me now, I think I am ready to sleep.'

The officer withdrew from the room, closing the door behind her. It shut softly, like a refrigerator. Lois and Israel settled back into their armchairs. The Dreamer went to the bed, slipped off her shoes, and eased herself under the doona. For a moment her body seemed to disappear into the restful brown patterns of her covering. Then she turned on her side and took the book from the bedside table. Enclosed in the book was a large photo of Lois and Israel. The Dreamer studied it carefully for several minutes before propping it against the lamp. She then opened the book and began to read. Lois and Israel, though nervously aware of every slight sound from the bed, adhered strictly to their orders and did not turn around. They continued to gaze blankly at the wall, ignoring even the sweat that they could feel stinging on their foreheads.

In the NDH Control Room crowds of people were gathered around the desks and tables. There was much talking but all of it quiet. From the speakers on the walls came only static.

'Would you do it?' a young lieutenant was asking a technician.

'No way,' the technician answered. 'No way. There are too many things I still want to do on Earth first. Anyhow, I don't like risks. What about you?'

'Don't know,' the lieutenant replied. 'I could do with a good tan.'

Lois and Israel heard the click behind them as the lamp went off. It seemed to them that the spread of darkness through the room was a slow, sluggish business that took many long seconds. But darkness it certainly was. They could barely see the wall. Israel suddenly remembered an old joke about the only safe time to travel to the Sun being night-time. He grinned wryly. As he did so he felt himself begin to move.

The quiet conversation in the Control Room suddenly stopped. The last, dead static from the speakers on the walls had been replaced by a low buzz; equally meaningless, but full of potential. Like everybody else the young lieutenant looked up at the speakers, as though by doing so he would hear better any sounds that emerged. A tense minute ticked away. Then there was a definite flicker from the speakers, a series of crackles, and at last a stammering human voice.

'Lois,' the technician said.

Everyone moved a step closer to the speakers.

'...and we don't know if we're moving or standing still. And we still don't know if you're hearing any of this. Over.'

The Chief Radio Officer, sweat soaking into his shirt, grabbed the microphone. 'Yes, just receiving you now, Icarus One. What is your situation please? Over.'

'Ah, good to hear your voice, NDH. It's hard to tell, but we think we're travelling at enormous speed ... The instruments certainly indicate that ...' There was a pause. 'Yes, confirming that, NDH. Israel confirms that we're now closing fast on the Sun ... We don't feel ...' A clatter of static drowned out her voice.

'Sleep patterns,' said someone.

'Might be near the chromosphere already,' the technician said.

'What's that word?' the young lieutenant asked.

The technician looked at him in amazement. 'Don't you know anything? What are you doing on this project?'

'I'm just Security.'

'Well, the chromosphere's a layer of atmosphere around the Sun. We think it's about 5000 ks thick, with a temperature of 20 000° Celsius.'

The lieutenant was impressed.

'That's some sauna! What's it like when you get through it?'

'Well, you come to the photosphere, which is the surface, if you can call it a surface. That's 6000°. But you'd take a couple of jumpers if you're going there, compared to the rest. We think it might be as much as 20 million degrees in the middle.'

'I lived in Garrett when I was a kid,' the lieutenant mused. 'In summer it'd get so hot we could fry pancakes on the footpath.'

There was another stutter from the speaker, and suddenly Lois' voice came through loudly and strongly.

'We're in the corona, we think, approaching the chromosphere. We're getting a heat reading of a million degrees outside. The light's very bright, as you can imagine. Over.'

'Are you having any problems? Over.'

'No! No!' There was no mistaking the excitement in her voice. 'The opposite: It's shimmering. We're flying through liquid heat. A waterfall of fire.'

'Describe your vehicle please. Over'

'It's a . . . a bubble. Oval shaped. So strong. We're sitting in chairs . . . really quite comfortable . . .'

*   *   *

In The Dreamer's bedroom there was no sound but the deep, slow breathing of the sleeping woman. The doona rose and fell slightly with each breath she took. The room seemed darker than ever. No one could have told that the shapeless mass of the doona concealed a human form. At one end of the room, facing the wall, were two empty armchairs.

A scientist in the Control Room was jotting calculations on the whiteboard during the periods when the radio was silent. In the background could be heard the Chief Radio Officer, speaking slowly and carefully into his large microphone.

'NDH to Icarus One. NDH to Icarus One. Come in, Icarus One. Over.'

'We think,' said the scientist, 'that these breaks in transmission happen when The Dreamer goes out of rapid-eye-movement and into deep sleep. As you know her periods of deep sleep are few, and of short duration, compared to the rest of us, anyway. But she still has them . . .'

The lieutenant, who was listening, said to the technician: 'What happens if she wakes up?'

The technician shrugged. 'That's the risk they take. But she's an experienced sleeper.'

The bubble hurtled on, like a marble thrown towards Niagara Falls. Its two occupants sat transfixed. The bubble was transparent, without allowing in heat. The light it admitted was the kind of dull red that comes with sunset on a cloud-scattered evening. Yet there was no mistaking the shocking brightness of the light, nor the horrifying heat of the star itself. The surface towards which they raced was not a surface at all but a raging ocean of red gases. Fumes, vapours and flames like gossamer fought and fought and fought in a madness of fire.

With difficulty Lois tore her eyes away, to look at Israel.

'Can we go through that and live?' she asked. 'Can we come back from here?'

He shrugged. 'If we go one way we can go the other.' But his shirt was drenched, and sweat was running down his face, so that he had to keep licking his upper lip.

The Dreamer was lying almost on her back, mouth slightly open. It was hot under the doona and the room was warm anyway. A fly had got in and was buzzing around the ceiling, hitting itself heavily against the peeling plaster. From behind a skirting-board came a faint scratching noise.

Israel's voice had taken over on the radio. 'We're seeing a perfect example of a sunspot now,' he reported. 'We're flying directly past it. It's a kind of heavy black fire, black flames. Like nothing we've seen before. Our instruments are registering a new kind of element, with new properties . . . Ahead of us is a huge bank of gas . . . a tornado as big and wide as the Himalayas, only brown and yellow and mottled . . . we're flying to the left of it.'

No one was stirring in the Control Room. Only the lieutenant moved suddenly, jumping, as a mouse ran over his foot.

'Damn mouse!' he said in surprise, to the technician, or to no one in particular.

'Yes,' the technician agreed, not taking his eyes off the speakers. 'They're in plague proportions at the moment. Getting cheekier every day.'

In the capsule, Israel heard something move behind him. He turned quickly, to see a pure white cat, with blue eyes, sitting gazing fondly out of the window. Israel tapped Lois on the shoulder and pointed towards the back of the bubble. She looked, and gasped, and then grinned at her partner.

'I guess this is the kind of thing they warned us about,' she said.

33

'Yes, I'm just surprised there haven't been more of them, and earlier. Even a Dreamer can't control everything.'

'It must be strange being a Dreamer. Because people actually get to see what's going on in your mind. Like we are now.'

'Did you bring any barley-sugar with you?' asked the cat. 'I get a little travel sick. And I've lost my dark glasses.'

'. . . enormous,' Lois reported. 'Thousands of square kilometres. They just blew right up. It was like a huge bubble coming to the surface, then the whole thing blew apart. I've never seen anything like it. Well, of course I haven't,' she added lamely. 'Anyway, we got sent spinning off for about a million ks. But when we could look back to where the explosion was, it was all normal again.'

The lieutenant looked out of the Control Room window at the Sun. It was too bright to look at directly: he had to shade his eyes. He wondered if these two people could really be up there. He turned back to the scene in the room. It was hot and crowded. He noticed a mousetrap under the desk, baited with a fragment of old cheese.

In the bedroom a mouse emerged from a crack at the end of the skirting-board. It ran across the carpet to the bed and sheltered under an end of the doona that was touching the floor. The Dreamer, in deep sleep once more, slept on.

'What was that?' Israel yelled.

'It's . . . oh, I don't know . . .' Lois gasped. 'Oh, what next? I hope she's not losing control.'

'What do you think it was?' Israel asked. 'I want to know if I saw it properly.'

'I think,' said Lois, 'I think it was a small tree on fire . . . and a man in robes. An old man . . . with a beard.'

'I concur,' said the cat.

'That's what I thought I saw,' said Israel.

The mouse was now sitting on top of the bed. It looked across the room, trembling faintly. Then, on feet that seemed to run on air, it scurried over the doona. It ran right across The Dreamer's face. With a scream of horror she awoke, sitting bolt upright, clutching her cheeks. Her eyes stared at the blank wall. She did not know what had woken her, but she knew something frightful had happened. The mouse, alarmed, had disappeared under the door. The Dreamer sat stiffly in the bed, looking at the two empty armchairs.

The lieutenant could not believe that screams so short could contain so much terror. They seemed to last much, much less than a second. The radio resumed its earlier empty mutter of static. Then it too fell silent.

MR PEMBERLEY CHECKS THE GATE

Morris Lurie

In the high stone vaulted entrance hall before the great door,
the great door of oldest oak stronger than any iron that had
once protected an ancient castle and borne witness to the
comings and goings of many kings, Mr Pemberley tallied the
time on his gold fobwatch with that on the face of the old
grandfather clock by the far wall, nodded, good, excellent,
eleven o'clock, eleven o'clock precisely, eleven o'clock on
the dot, donned his overcoat and his muffler and his favourite soft tweed cap, and then took up, first, in his left hand, his
flashlight, tested it – yes, all in order, the beam strong and
sharp and true – and then, in his right hand, his stout stick of
black mahogany with the carved white ivory grip in the

37

shape of a crouched tiger, and then, thus dressed and pre-pared and equipped, stepped out, as he did every night at exactly this time, to check the gate. The great door closed behind him with a sound of banks. The stick was for the bears.

Mr Pemberley stood stock-still outside in the night.

And first, as he did every night, Mr Pemberley sniffed, a great deep sniff filling his sharp nose with the smell of trees and lawns and flowers and bushes, of thick leaf mould and rich black soil, of things wet, of things growing, and all his, every single leaf, every single spot of soil, every single bud and blade of grass, Pemberley property, Pemberley land, the rich smell of ownership, mine, all mine.

'Ah!' said Mr Pemberley.

And then, as he did every night, Mr Pemberley stared, a great deep stare filling his sharp eyes with the canopy of the sky vast overhead, the clear night sky unsullied by fumes of industry or traffic, by smokes, by smogs, the sky rich with stars and ablaze with moon, and all beaming down just for him staring up, Pemberley heavens, Pemberley lights, the rich blaze of ownership, mine, all mine.

'Ah!' said Mr Pemberley.

Now Mr Pemberley pointed his sharp nose and his sharp eyes straight ahead, and with his grip firm on his flashlight in one hand and on his stout stick in the other he stepped out onto the white gravel of the long driveway to the gate lit by the blazing moon like a white road through his gardens dark on either side, and with his stout stick stabbing the gravel too at every second step *crunch! crunch!* he began.

Mr Pemberley, it should be said, was rich. He was very rich. In the Pemberley garage, for instance, there were, at last count, some ninety-two vehicles, including a fire engine, a bright red double-decker British bus, four personal heli-copters and a hydrofoil, as well as the usual limousines, racers and sedans. (The tractors, trucks, earth-movers and cranes were in a separate garage.)

But Mr Pemberley was richer than vehicles, than merely vehicles.

'Ah, the shops!' said Mr Pemberley, passing on his left a dark thicket of tall firs.

'Ah, the school!' said Mr Pemberley, passing on his right his roses growing in elegant rows.

'Ah, the Town Hall!' said Mr Pemberley, his sharp eyes swinging to the rolling lawn smooth as velvet where once the Town Hall had stood.

Crunch! Crunch! went Mr Pemberley's satisfied shoes on the moon-white gravel drive.

Stab! Stab! went Mr Pemberley's ivory and mahogany stout stick.

Oh, he was rich all right, was Mr Pemberley. He was richer than rich. Mr Pemberley was rich beyond counting, beyond figures, beyond numbers, beyond even the descriptive power of words.

Mr Pemberley was so gloriously hugely richly rich that where he strode now along the driveway, shoes crunching on the gravel to check the gate, had once been a suburb, a whole suburb, an entire suburb of houses and streets and roads and lanes and paths and roundabouts, and Mr Pemberley had bought it all.

'Everything!' said Mr Pemberley.

Yes, even the shops, even the school, even the Town Hall too.

'Everything!' said Mr Pemberley.

He'd bought the railway station, and rolled up all the line.

He'd bought the library, and thrown away all the books.

'Everything!' said Mr Pemberley.

Yes, he'd bought it all, every brick, every building, every single last thing, and crunched and crumbled it all down, and had constructed instead a great park of lakes and lawns and woods and waterfalls and his own golf course and his own private zoo and even his own racing road to roar along in his clanging fire engine (when he was in the mood), and in the middle of it all he had put his grand house, and around it all the highest wall with just the one safe strong iron gate the only way in and the only way out which every night at exactly eleven o'clock Mr Pemberly strode from his house to check.

'Exactly!' said Mr Pemberley.

Now a rainforest hove into view, a dense, lush jungle of giant ferns and thick creepers and sturdy bamboos and lofty palms, with the soft sound of water running somewhere through, all bathed by the moon.

'Ah, Miss Rafferty!' said Mr Pemberley.

And Mr Pemberley smiled.

Mr Pemberley chuckled.

Mr Pemberley laughed out loud.

'Ha ha!' laughed Mr Pemberley, stabbing the gravel with his stick.

For Miss Rafferty had been the one, the only one, who had refused to sell.

Refused and refused and refused.

'Never!' she had said. 'Not for millions! Not for anything! I will never sell you my house and home! Never! Not ever! Not even if I'm the last person in the last house left in the whole suburb!'

And she was.

The only remaining house.

For a whole year.

Until Mr Pemberley installed his private zoo right next door to her.

And the next morning Miss Rafferty opened her bedroom curtains and staring in at her were the small-eyed, wet-snouted, yellow-fanged faces of bears.

'I'm off!' shrieked Miss Rafferty. 'I've gone! I'm out!' fleeing from her house, still in her nightie, not even bothering to pack.

'Good-bye, Miss Rafferty!' said Mr Pemberley, crunching on the gravel.

And whisked in a rainforest where once her house had stood.

'Good-bye!'

Except now the bears had somehow got loose.

And were roaming.

Lurking.

Somewhere in the great dark park.

Mr Pemberley gripped tighter his flashlight, gripped harder his stout mahogany stick.

His sharp nose sniffed, his sharp eyes searched, his sharp ears strained for the slightest sound in the vast theatre of the night.

Anything?

Nothing.

'Good!' said Mr Pemberley.

Ah, and here was the gate, the gate at last, the gate Mr Pemberley had come to check.

'Good!' said Mr Pemberley.

Mr Pemberley put down his flashlight, rested his stick.

Now, as he did every night, gripping the bars of mighty iron with both hands, the mighty iron spiked on top and bolted and padlocked and its two halves wound round and round with the strongest chain, Mr Pemberley tested it, he shook it, he rattled it as hard as he possibly could.

The mighty gate stood, as strong as ever, as strong as before.

All locked.

All secure.

All safe.

'Good!' said Mr Pemberley.

And now this happened, as it did every night.

Mr Pemberley looked through the gate, looked for a long moment through its bars and past its bolts and padlocks and wound-around chain, at the world beyond, and saw there, as he did every night, the lights of streets and the shapes of houses, and the people inside asleep, at peace in the night, and Mr Pemberley felt, as he did every night, somehow wistful.

Could it be, even sad?

'But why?' said Mr Pemberley. 'I have everything!'

The houses beyond the gate said nothing.

'Ha!' said Mr Pemberley.

And Mr Pemberley gave his gate one last good strong rattle, and then picked up his flashlight and his stick, and turned, and *crunch! crunch!* started firmly back.

'Ha!' said Mr Pemberley.

Almost at once there was a stir in the bushes.

Mr Pemberley flashed the flashlight.

Now the stir was on the other side.

Mr Pemberley flashed again.

The moon had set in the night sky, and now Mr Pemberley saw that where the driveway had been like a white road through his garden dark on either side, now it was not, now it was quite dark too, with only the jumping beam of his flashlight and the hard crunching of the gravel under his feet to tell Mr Pemberley where he was.

Another stir!

The rainforest!

There was something in the rainforest!

The flashlight almost jumped from Mr Pemberley's hand.

Or was it a leaf?

Only a leaf?

Only a leaf shining in all that darkness and wetness and blackness?

'Don't run!' said Mr Pemberley.

Mr Pemberley's knuckles were white on the stout stick in his right hand, as white as the carved white crouched tiger he gripped for dear life.

And the house still so far away.

'Don't run!' said Mr Pemberley.

Now it was louder.

Closer.

A crashing in the bushes in Mr Pemberley's great park loud and close on either side.

'Don't run!' said Mr Pemberley, and, as he did every night, Mr Pemberley ran –

He ran and ran and ran.

The bushes crashing closer all around –

And ran and ran and ran.

And when he almost couldn't run any more –

There was the house with its great door of oldest oak stronger than any iron and –

Slam!

He was inside!

And the last sound you will hear in this story is the whirring of the old grandfather clock in the entrance hall by the far wall about to strike.

'Goodness,' said Mr Pemberley. 'It's almost time to get up!'

NIGHT OF PASSAGE
Lee Harding

When they came in sight of the city, Brin left the rest of the party behind and continued on alone.

The Elders settled down to wait. They prayed for her safe return, then drank wine and smoked ceremonial pipes and chanted the old songs. This also was part of the ritual, and they would keep it up without pause until she returned.

Brin made good time across the open ground, her natural environment. Crouching low so her dark skin merged with the sunburned grass, she moved with a lithe step. Later, the going would not be so easy.

The time was late afternoon and she planned to reach the outskirts of the city before dusk. She had no desire to enter this unknown labyrinth until daylight waned, and would bide her time until twilight, when the gathering darkness would afford her cover.

When she considered the dangers that lay ahead her fear returned, but if she survived this long night of Passage tomorrow she would be a woman, and privy to the mysteries of her clan. Such was the nature of her trial.

She paused to take stock of her surroundings. Choosing a suitable tree, she quickly scaled it and settled down high up among the sweet-scented branches to await the dusk.

Nothing moved on the landscape. A swollen orange sun dipped slowly out of sight behind the ramparts of the distant city, the gaunt buildings silhouetted against the sunset like the escarpment of some forbidding mountain range. In the distance she imagined she could hear the ritual chanting of the Elders, wafted to her on the shoulders of the night-wind. She felt lonely and isolated, but she had no wish to turn back. Not when she had come so far.

The world gradually darkened. When the first wan stars appeared overhead she clasped both hands together and whispered the Prayer of Passage, remembering home and family and brother Mark, who would make his run next summer. What tales they would share when he became a man! This done, she climbed down from her perch and set off at a brisk pace on the next stage of her journey.

As she moved closer to the city, the fields became hazardous underfoot. They were littered with relics of the Old Ones and avoiding them made for slow progress. Brin angled towards the old road, confident this would lead her to the heart of the city, yet unwilling to betray herself by stepping onto it. Instead she followed the road at a discreet distance, crouching low so her fingers brushed the ground. Her senses ranged far ahead, alert for the slightest sound that would signal the presence of predators on this no-man's-land between the city and the open country. Occasionally the ruins of an ancient wheeled vehicle loomed before her and she gave these a wide berth. It was known that wild dogs and other dangerous animals used these hulks for shelter, and she had no desire to arouse their curiosity.

Her right hand never strayed far from the knife sheathed at her waist and her left hand clutched the small bag of stones jostling against her thigh. Her body was covered with a rime of sweat, but she had no inkling of fatigue. She was no stranger to long treks, although this was the most hazardous she had undertaken. But despite her fears she drew courage from knowing that this night would conclude her quest for womanhood and provide a bridge between her childhood and the person she was destined to become. It was a long-established ritual of her people.

Tonight the sky was clear and there would be a full moon to guide her. These were auspicious omens. The city would be a maze of darkness and the light of heaven her only ally; and when she arrived at the outskirts of the city several hours would remain before she reached the centre. This road would lead her there, to be sure, but for safety she would hug the shadows and side-streets and use the darkness to conceal her presence. If she made good time she hoped to reach her goal before midnight, then find somewhere safe to remain until morning. When dawn arrived she would select her trophy – this, too, was part of the ritual – and depart in haste before the daylight betrayed her.

She paused when she reached the outskirts of the city. The stark contours of the squat buildings were a jangling discord in her mind. They were so different from the homes of her people, which everywhere blended harmoniously with their surroundings. She felt a twinge of dread standing so close to strangeness but steeled herself to move closer, for she had need of the protective shadows.

In this devious way did she enter the abandoned city, a slender figure moving deeper into darkness, her senses alert for any sign of danger. Even now, so long after The Fall, it was known that the city was not entirely deserted. Strange stories had been told by previous initiates, although one could never be sure how much was fact and how much was mere fancy, intensified by fear and anxiety. But it was sobering to recall the youngsters who had failed to return from their night of Passage. Surely this was proof that the dangers still lurked in the city.

Much of what Brin knew about the city was either legend or hearsay, from which some useful facts could be gleaned. It seemed likely that wild dogs prowled the concrete canyons and it was assumed they would be more dangerous than their counterparts in the open country. Some experts insisted that animals of the plain would not dare venture inside the city, for fear of what they might find there. Brin was not prepared to take chances. She was determined to survive her night of Passage and attain her majority, although she wished for a companion to shore up her courage. It was customary for groups of two or three to make their run together, but this summer she was the only youngster to celebrate her fifteenth birthday and, as a consequence, was expected to make her run alone.

She hurried along the crumbling footpaths, nimbly avoiding a variety of obstructions. The silence was strained and unnatural, unlike the silence of the open country, where small sounds were always present. But as her senses grew more attuned to these unfamiliar surroundings she realised that the silence was not as absolute as she had first thought. Far off, near the centre of the city, she heard faintly the sorrowful howl of some melancholy animal. Her scalp prickled with apprehension. She was too far from the source of the sound to be sure, but it reminded her of some disconsolate beast baying its loneliness to the night sky. She unsheathed her knife in preparedness as she moved deeper into the labyrinth.

The city stank. She had expected this, yet even so she was

unprepared for the way the rank odour clung like a shroud. A great many people had perished here in Olden Times and the air was heavy with the burden of their passing. Perhaps in the patience of time this odour would be banished from the city by tireless winds and cleansing rains, but for now it remained trapped by the tall buildings, and this made her task even more unpleasant. The streets had a deep layer of dust that soon covered her skin and worked its way into her eyes and down her throat. She was afraid she might cough and several times had to stifle a sneeze, knowing the sound would reverberate catastrophically in these surroundings and betray her presence.

Brin watched the moon rise, transforming the road into a ribbon of light cutting a broad swathe through the darkness. This encouraged her to move faster, but it also made her more vulnerable. As she approached the centre of the city the forlorn baying grew more pronounced. There seemed to be more than one animal, spread over a wide area, tossing their loneliness back and forth across the rooftops. The doleful sound honed her fear and made her wonder how effective her knife would be against a determined predator. Bad luck for her if the dogs roamed in packs ...

The buildings around her looked different now. They were no longer simple dwellings but resembled storage silos. Yet even so, the tallest was no more than five storeys. She checked the levels carefully, the shattered windows gaping like rows of broken teeth, and found five less than the ten required by the rules of Passage. There was no question of cheating and choosing a hideout some distance from the centre, because guilt would betray her when she faced the Elders. Disgrace would follow and the mysteries of her clan would remain closed to her. She could not and would not evade her responsibilities. The only way out was forward.

The moon rose higher, drawing a soft silver shawl over the city. Brin thought about the moon, how people had lived there long ago in their marvellous domed cities, before The Fall cut them off from Earth like divers deprived of air. Were they still there, she wondered, their dead eyes focused forever on the slowly turning Earth?

She stopped and rubbed sweaty hands on her thighs. What if the dust underfoot was all that remained of the people who had lived here long ago, a grim residue tossed and spread around by the gale-force winds that had scoured these streets for centuries?

The idea was disturbing. She scolded herself and thought, 'This is mere fancy.' Then she looked nervously around as though expecting some grey old ghost to sneak up from behind and tap her on the shoulder. But no such phantom appeared to mock her progress. There was only the doleful cry of lonely animals baying at the moon to sharpen her wits.

The road rose unexpectedly from ground level to become an elevated highway. Tempting though this was, Brin chose to scurry from shadow to deeper shadow between the crumbling pillars that still supported the structure. The road stretched above her like an enormous arm outflung against the stars. Further on, when the road sloped back to level ground again, she moved away from its protective shadows and hugged the flat sides of buildings. She was tiring now, but the end of her journey was in sight. The buildings either side were higher now, and the animal howling was louder.

The streets of the city were choked with derelict vehicles left behind by the Old Ones, some lying overturned and others with wheels buried in the pervasive dust like insects trapped in honey. Their diversity astonished her. Never before had she seen so many ancient artefacts crowded together, and this alone made her trek worthwhile. Legend maintained that The Fall happened so quickly people scarcely had time to save themselves, the Old World collapsing so completely that hardly anyone survived. Afterwards, great plagues had ravaged the world and left only a few precious havens untouched. But this was hearsay. Who could say with certainty what had caused The Fall and changed the face of the Earth for ever?

Brin skidded to a stop. Her pulse was racing and she was breathing heavily, but there were no other signs of strain after her long run. Grey buildings soared all around her, their topmost levels lost in darkness. She had reached the centre at last, where she must make her stand and await the dawn. But which building offered the best cover?

The doleful baying seemed everywhere now. Were the dogs closing in? she wondered. Or had anxiety overtaken her senses? She counted the rows of gaping windows on the building opposite and saw it would suffice. It was a good deal higher than the ten storeys demanded by the rules of Passage.

She crossed the street, weaving her way through a tangle of derelict vehicles. On the other side she paused, confronted by a shattered wall of glass. Great shards littered the footpath, where two wheeled vehicles had plunged their blunt snouts through the shopfront. Bodies were strewn around inside the building and this seemed odd. How could bodies be so remarkably well preserved after so long?

She took a step closer and peered into the store, sighing with relief when she realised these were not real people. They were toppled statues. The moonlight had deceived her into thinking them human. Some stood in frozen tableaux with arms extended in a parody of human gesture, their painted eyes devoid of feeling; others were sprawled on the floor in awkward postures. Scraps of fibre that might once have been cloth clung to their limbs, reminding her of the dolls she had kept as a child.

She stepped cautiously through the shattered window. Inside the huge store the darkness was almost palpable and she paused to allow time for her senses to adjust to these new surroundings. Row after row of deep shelves stretched away from her and disappeared into the deeper darkness at

51

the back of the store. The nearest were still filled with merchandise, glass and metal containers with faded labels displaying familiar fruit or vegetables.

Brin was fascinated. What an abundance of trophies to choose from! She remembered the silver case Tony had brought back from his run, the fascia decorated with numerals and the panel that gaped open when a switch was pressed like a mouth demanding to be fed. The Elders had regarded this suspiciously at first, before they chanted the Song of Internment and buried the artefact in the ground. She was determined to select something that would astound The Elders and impress her family and friends. But this could wait until morning. Her priority was to find a safe place for the night.

She hunkered down in a far corner of the store, her back to the wall and with a clear view of the street outside. The baying had moved to another part of the city and this made her feel easier; perhaps the pack would move even further away. But just as she allowed herself to relax the silence was broken by the most mournful howl she had ever heard. This seemed very close indeed. She fingered her knife nervously – dawn seemed far away – and untied the pouch cinched to her belt. She opened this and drew out her stones, arranging them on the floor within easy reach. Knife-work could be messy and was often unnecessary. A stone could fell even the largest adversary if the thrower's aim was sure.

Fortunately, the sound was not repeated, and after a while she allowed herself to relax again. The tension ebbed from her body and she at last succumbed to weariness. Eventually she slept, secure with a hunter's knowledge that her senses would alert her to any danger. And while she slept she dreamed of home, of family and friends and the valley she loved. She dreamed how the sun illuminated every corner of their lives, how it charmed the seeds from the soil and nourished the crops. How the river sparkled on long summer afternoons . . .

She woke when the first faint light of dawn crept in through the shattered windows of the store . . . and realised she was not alone.

She was instantly on guard, senses alert for any sound. She clasped the knife in her right hand while her left gripped a throwing stone, ready to defend herself.

What sound had disturbed her? What danger had crept into her dreams and nudged her awake? Her keen eyes probed the surrounding darkness, looking for some clue. Her heart hammered in her breast like a frightened bird beating wildly at its cage. She waited, and after a while heard a faint creeping sound. Something moved on her right. She could make out a dark shape lurking there, shuffling about the store with a furtiveness unlike any animal she knew.

'Lord Sun, protect me,' she whispered.

So far the creature was unaware of her presence, but when it did sense her she would face the supreme test of Passage. If she survived, her majority was assured. If she did not, her people would mourn her, as they had mourned others who had not returned from the city.

She could hear the creature groping around in the darkness, its muffled breathing moving closer to her hideaway as it shuffled past the shelves. Was it searching for food? she wondered. But what sort of animal grubbed around in the ruins of this store? Her fear gave way to curiosity. Brin had faith in her knife and her skill with the stones and she edged forward slightly, hoping for a better glimpse of the intruder. She saw a dim shape hovering around a pyramid of food cans. She drew her breath in sharply. The creature was hunched over with its back to her and was much bigger than she had anticipated.

Brin hesitated. Now was the time to make good her escape.

She didn't fancy staying crouched in her corner, waiting for the creature to discover her and block her escape route. She had no idea how fast it could move, but she was the fastest runner in the valley and was confident she could out-distance any pursuer – except a marauding dog-pack.

She calculated the distance between herself and the intruder, then the distance between herself and the street. There was no sense delaying her break a moment longer. The time to make her move was *now*, while the creature was occupied. But what about her trophy? She couldn't leave empty-handed.

At this precise moment she sneezed. Afterwards, she would never be sure what had provoked the sudden parox-ysm, whether it was a consequence of the dust she had inhaled or if subconsciously she had wished to challenge the intruder. Whatever the reason, the result was spectacular.

The creature let out a roar and swung around as though it had been struck, its huge arms toppling merchandise from the shelves as they spread wide in a defiant gesture of aggression. When it saw her crouched in the half-light it let loose a cry so terrifying that Brin promptly jumped to her feet, legs braced firmly as she assumed a defensive stance. For she recognised in the creature's cry the same disturbing howl she had heard during the night. *This* was the creature she had sought to avoid. No wild dog after all, but something else . . .

The creature confronting her was *huge* and vaguely man-like. Coarse white hair stood out from his head like wire and a grizzled beard straggled down past his waist. The man was naked, save for a small garment loosely tied around his loins, and under the grime his skin was the same pallid colour as the belly of a fish. There was a crazed look in his wild eyes and more menace in his emaciated frame than Brin had ever seen.

Twenty paces separated them. The creature gave another

dreadful cry and launched itself towards her; enormous hands clawing the air and eyes blazing with an unreasonable hatred. Brin did not hesitate. The creature presented an easy target. She faced the charge coolly, eyeing the man with shrewd calculation. She waited until he had closed half the distance between them, then with a grim smile raised her left hand in a blur of speed. The stone flew from her fingers and struck the wild white man hard in the centre of the forehead. The creature staggered to a stop, eyes rolling heavenwards while it clawed at its head with both hands. She had another stone ready, but this was not necessary. The creature coughed once and collapsed to the floor without making another sound.

Brin waited a few moments, out of caution, but the creature did not stir. Her aim had been true and the stone had knocked him unconscious. She moved closer and looked down in wonder at the body, embedding the image in her memory for future reference. Wild white hair framed the creature's head like a crinkled halo, his chest rose and fell steadily from his breathing and she suspected it would be some time before he regained consciousness. By then she would be well clear of the city and on her way home.

Early morning sunlight filtered into the store. This was no time for musing. She remembered her trophy and wavered for a moment, uncertain. She looked again at the unconscious wild man and making her decision, leaned forward and struck swiftly with her knife. And in one lithe movement she was away and heading for the street.

She fled from the city as though all the wild dogs in the world were snapping at her heels, hugging the shadows and praying she would not be seen by other predators, detouring down side streets and alleyways when the open spaces made her conspicuous and choking back the rising clouds of dust. Several times she imagined the dreadful baying sound behind her and quickened her pace. But no predators approached her, and if any followed she out-distanced them easily.

She was surprised when the return journey was accomplished without incident. She grew light-headed and flushed with her success and found time to marvel at the enormous size of the city and the great distances separating the wild white people who lived there, subsisting on the left-overs of their ancestors and ignorant of their former glory.

Her trophy swung lightly from her belt and did not impede her progress. She ran until she was exhausted, until the outskirts of the city were far behind and the green of the open country was spread before her. Only then did she feel secure enough to ease her pace.

The Elders were waiting. Ritual required them to welcome her solemnly, yet their expressions betrayed how delighted they were to see her return safe and sound. She approached their camp with a jaunty step, proud of her accomplishment and only now appreciating the audacity of her adventure. Her long night was over and her Passage had been successful.

They acknowledged her safe return with customary dignity, which also was part of the ritual. Then they carefully examined her body for wounds and abrasions and were relieved when they found none. They inspected the crust of dried sweat and dust that covered her from head to foot and murmured their approval.

Brin smiled triumphantly as she held out her trophy. The Eldest accepted it nervously and examined the long strands of white hair in wonderment. The others crowded closer to examine her prize, their faces filled with awe. Then they each in turn examined the thatch of hair she had severed from the unconscious wild man and nodded their approval. The inspection complete, they regarded her with admiration and a new respect. No initiate had ever returned from the city with such a bizarre prize.

The trophy was returned to the Eldest, who proceeded to wrap it in a ceremonial cloth and tuck it away in the special basket designed for the purpose. Then he motioned for the group to move off. They began the slow, measured trek that would take them back to the valley, where three days hence they would celebrate her safe return and declare her Passage complete.

And from their proud and dignified expressions Brin knew she had at last achieved her majority.

AUNT MILLICENT
Mary Steele

'I,' said Angelica Tonks, grandly, 'have eight uncles and eleven aunts.'

Angelica Tonks had more of most things than anyone else. She held the class record for pairs of fashion sneakers and Derwent pencil sets, and her pocket-money supply was endless. Now, it seemed, she also had the largest uncle-and-aunt collection in town. Her classmates squirmed and made faces at each other. *Awful* Angelica Tonks.

Mr Wilfred Starling dusted the chalk from his bony hands and sighed. 'Well, Angelica, aren't you a lucky one to have nineteen uncles and aunts. You'll just have to choose the most interesting one to write about, won't you?'

'But they're *all* interesting,' objected Angelica. 'The Tonks family is a wonderfully interesting family, you know. It will be terribly hard to choose just one.'

There were more squirms. The class was fed up with the wonderfully interesting Tonks family. In fact, Mr Wilfred Starling nearly screamed. He just managed to swallow his exasperation, which sank down to form a hard bubble in his stomach. Straightening his thin shoulders, he said, 'Right, everyone, copy down this week's homework assignment from the board. And remember, Angelica, a pen-portrait of just *one* aunt or uncle is all I want. Just *one*.' *Please not a whole gallery of tedious and terrible Tonkses*, he thought to himself.

The class began to write. Jamie Nutbeam, sitting behind Angelica, leaned forward and hissed, 'If the rest of your family is so *wonderfully interesting*, they must be a big improvement on you, Honky! And, anyway, I bet the aunt I write about will beat any of yours!'

'I bet she won't,' Angelica hissed back. 'She'll be so *boring*. What's her name, this boring aunt?'

Jamie finished copying and put down his pen. 'Aunt Millicent, and she's pretty special.'

'Millicent!' scoffed Angelica. 'What a name! No one's called Millicent these days!'

'QUIET, you two!' barked Mr Starling, massaging his stomach, 'and start tidying up, everyone – it's time for the bell.' *Oh bliss*, he thought.

As the classroom emptied, Jamie lingered behind.

'What is it, Jamie?' asked Mr Starling wearily, piling his books and papers together and trying not to burp.

'Well, the trouble is I haven't any aunts or uncles to do a portrait of,' said Jamie, turning rather red, 'so is it all right if I make one up? An aunt?'

'Oh, I see! Well, in that case ... yes, perfectly all right,' replied Mr Starling. He gazed rather sadly out the window. 'The most interesting characters in the world are usually the made-up ones, you know, Jamie. Think of Sherlock Holmes and Alice and Dr Who and Indiana Jones . . .'

Jamie interrupted. 'Does anyone need to know I've made her up? This aunt?'

'Well, *I* won't say anything,' promised Mr Starling. 'It's for you to make her seem real so we all believe in her. You go home and see what you can dream up.'

'She has a name already,' Jamie called back as he left the room. 'She's Aunt Millicent.'

Aunt Millicent Nutbeam! The hard bubble in Mr Starling's stomach began to melt away.

That evening, Jamie Nutbeam said to his family at large, 'Did you know that awful Angelica Tonks has eight uncles and eleven aunts?'

'Well, everybody knows that they're a big family,' replied his mother.

'Prolific, I'd call it,' grunted Jamie's father from behind his newspaper.

'Yes, dear – prolific. Now, Mrs Tonks was a Miss Blizzard,' continued Mrs Nutbeam, 'and there are lots of Blizzards around here as well as Tonkses, all related, no doubt. But fancy nineteen! Who told you there were nineteen, Jamie?'

'She did – old Honky Tonks herself. She told the whole class *and* Mr Starling – boasting away as usual. She's a *pill*.' Jamie was jotting things on paper as he talked. 'We have to write a pen-portrait of an aunt or uncle for homework, and Honky can't decide which one to do because they're all so *wonderfully interesting*, she says. Urk!' He paused and then added, 'I'm doing Aunt Millicent.'

Jamie's father peered over the top of his newspaper. 'Aunt who?'

'Who's Aunt Millicent?' demanded Jamie's sister, Nerissa.

'You haven't got an Aunt Millicent,' said his mother. 'You haven't any aunts at all, *or* uncles, for that matter.'

'I *know* I haven't,' Jamie snapped. 'It's *hopeless* belonging to a nuclear family! It's unfair – I mean, awful Honky has nineteen aunts and uncles and Nerissa and I haven't got any, not one.' Jamie ground the pencil between his teeth.

'You won't have any teeth either, if you munch pencils like that,' remarked his father, who was a dentist.

Jamie glowered, spitting out wet splinters.

'Anyway, he's right,' announced Nerissa. 'It would be great to have even one aunt or uncle. Then we might have some cousins, too. Everyone else has cousins. Angelica Tonks probably has about a hundred-and-twenty-seven.'

'Well, I'm sorry,' sighed Mrs Nutbeam, 'but your father and I are both "onlys" and there's nothing we can do about that, is there? Not a thing! Now, what's all this about an Aunt Millicent?'

'Oh, it's okay,' grumbled her son. 'Mr Starling said to write about *an* aunt or uncle, not exactly *my* aunt or uncle. He says I can invent one.'

'Will you explain that she's not real?' asked Nerissa, doubtfully.

'Mr Starling says I don't have to, and he's not going to tell. He says I have to make people believe that she *is* real. Anyway, I don't want Honky Tonks to know that she's made up, because Aunt Millicent is going to be amazing – much better than any of those boring Tonkses. It's time Honky was taken down a peg or two.'

Dr Nutbeam quite understood how Jamie felt. From time to time Angelica Tonks visited his dentist's chair. She would brag about her 'perfect' teeth if there was nothing to be fixed, but if she needed a filling her shrieks of 'agony' would upset everyone in the waiting room and Mrs Tonks would call Dr Nutbeam a *brute*. He was often tempted to give Angelica a general anaesthetic and post her home in a large jiffy bag.

Now he folded his newspaper; Jamie's project sounded rather fun. 'Right, Jamie,' he said, 'tell us about Aunt Millicent and let us get some facts straight. Is she my sister, or Mum's? We must get that settled to start with.'

'I can't decide,' frowned Jamie. 'What do you think?'

'She'd better be your sister, dear,' said Mrs Nutbeam calmly to her husband. 'I grew up here and everyone knows I was an only child, but you came from another town. You're more mysterious.'

Dr Nutbeam looked pleased. 'Mm ... mm. That's nice ... having a sister, I mean. Is she younger than me?'

'No, older,' said Jamie.

'Where does she live?' asked Nerissa. 'Has she a family of her own? Lots of cousins for us?'

'No way – she hasn't time for all that sort of thing. And she doesn't live anywhere in particular.'

Mrs Nutbeam looked puzzled. 'What *do* you mean, dear? What does Auntie Millicent do, exactly?'

'She's an explorer,' said Jamie, proudly. 'She works for foreign governments, and she's terribly busy – flat out.'

There was something of a pause. Then Dr Nutbeam said, 'Ah,' and stroked his bald patch. 'That explains why we haven't seen her for so long.'

'What does she explore?' demanded Nerissa. 'Is there anything left in the world to look for?'

Jamie was beginning to feel a bit rushed. 'Well, I'm not sure yet, but foreign governments need people like her to search for water in deserts and rich mineral deposits and endangered species and things ... you know.'

Nerissa lay on the floor with her eyes closed and began to imagine her new aunt slashing a path through tangled jungle vines, searching for a rare species of dark blue frog. The mosquitoes were savage. The leeches were huge and bloated. Aunt Millicent's machete was razor sharp ...

'This is all very unexpected,' murmured Mrs Nutbeam, 'to have a sister-in-law who is an explorer, I mean. I wonder how you get started in that sort of career?' Her own job as an assistant in an antique and curio shop suddenly seemed rather drab.

Dr Nutbeam was staring at the wall. In his mind's eye he clearly saw his sister on a swaying rope suspension bridge above a terrifying ravine. She was leading a band of native bearers to the other side. How much more adventurous, he thought, than drilling little holes in people's teeth. He wrenched his gaze back to Jamie and asked, 'Do we know what Millie is actually exploring at present?'

Jamie munched his pencil for a moment and then said, 'She's in Africa, somewhere near the middle, but I'm not sure where, exactly.'

'In the middle of Africa, is she?' echoed Dr Nutbeam. 'Mm ... then it wouldn't surprise me if she were in the Cameroons. There's a lot of dense forest in the Cameroons, you know.'

'I thought Cameroons were things to eat,' frowned Nerissa. 'Sort of coconut biscuits.'

'No, no, dear, those are macaroons,' said her mother.

'*They're* bad for your teeth, too,' remarked her father, absently, 'like eating pencils.'

Jamie fetched the atlas and found a map of Africa. His father stood behind him, peering at it. 'There it is, in the middle on the left-hand side, just under the bump.'

'It's called Cameroon here,' Jamie said. 'Just one of them.'

'Well, there's East Cameroon and West Cameroon, see,' pointed his father, 'and sometimes you lump them together and call them Cameroons. Look – here's the equator just to the south, so it must be pretty hot and steamy at sea-level.'

'Poor Millicent,' sighed Mrs Nutbeam. 'I do hope her feet don't swell in the heat, with all that walking.'

Jamie examined the map closely. 'That's peculiar – the north border of the Cameroons seems to be floating in a big lake ... um, Lake Chad ... it looks all swampy, with funny dotted lines and things. I bet that bit needs exploring.

They've probably lost their border in the mud and Aunt Millicent could be on an expedition to find it.'

'Is she all by herself?' asked Nerissa. 'I'd be scared in a place like that.'

'Of course she's not by herself,' snorted Jamie. 'She works for a foreign government, don't forget, and she'd have a whole support team of porters and cooks and scientists and things.'

'She must be an expert at something herself, don't you think?' suggested Mrs Nutbeam. 'I would imagine that she's a surveyor.'

'Yes, she'd use one of those instruments you look through, on legs,' added Nerissa.

'You mean a theodolite, dim-wit,' answered her brother.

'She'd certainly need one of those, if she's measuring angles and distances and drawing maps,' agreed Dr Nutbeam. 'My word, what a clever old sister I have!'

'I wonder if she was good at Geography at school?' said Nerissa.

'Well, you'll be able to ask Grandma tomorrow. She's coming for her winter visit, remember?'

'Oh help! What'll Grandma *say*?' gasped Jamie. 'Do you think she'll mind? I mean – we've invented a daughter for her without asking!'

'I shouldn't think she'd mind,' said his mother. 'We'll break the news to her carefully and see how she takes it.'

Grandma Nutbeam, as it turned out, was delighted.

'How exciting!' she exclaimed. 'I always wanted a daughter, and it's been very lonely since Grandpa died. Now I'll have a new interest! Just show me on the map where Millicent is at the moment, please dear.'

Jamie pointed to the dotted lines in swampy Lake Chad near the top end of the Cameroons, and Grandma stared in astonishment.

'Gracious heaven! What an extraordinary place to go to, the silly girl! I hope she's remembered her quinine tablets. Millicent was never very good at looking after herself, you know. Let me see – I think I'll get some wool tomorrow and knit her some good stout hiking socks.'

Jamie blinked. 'There's no need to do that, Grandma. She's not really real, you know.'

'Well, she'll be more real to me if I make her some socks,' Grandma declared.

'Wouldn't they be rather hot in the Cameroons?' objected Nerissa. 'It's awfully near the equator, don't forget.'

'Woollen socks are best in any climate,' said Grandma firmly. 'They breathe.'

'Now, Mother,' interrupted Dr Nutbeam, 'you can tell us what Millicent was like as a girl. I can't remember her very well, as she was so much older than me, but I have a feeling that she ran away from home a lot.'

Grandma pondered a moment. 'Now that you mention it, she did. She did indeed. I thought we'd have to chain her up sometimes! We lived near the edge of town, you'll remember, and Millie would look out towards the paddocks and hills and say that she wanted to know what was over the horizon, or where the birds were flying to, or where the clouds came from behind the hills. We never knew where she'd be off to next – but she certainly ended up in the right job! I'm so glad she became an explorer. If I were a bit younger and had better feet, I might even go and join her. It would be most interesting to see the Cameroons. It's full of monkeys, I believe.'

'Was Aunt Millicent good at Geography at school?' Nerissa remembered to ask.

'Let me think – yes, she must have been because one year she won a prize for it, and the prize was a book called *Lives of the Great Explorers*.'

'Well, there you are,' remarked Mrs Nutbeam. 'That's probably how it all started.'

Next day, Grandma Nutbeam began to knit a pair of explorer's socks. She decided on khaki with dark blue stripes round the top.

Angelica Tonks had found it so difficult to select one of the nineteen aunts and uncles, that her pen-portrait was left until the very last minute and then scrawled out in a great hurry. She had finally chosen Aunt Daisy Blizzard, Mrs Tonks's eldest sister.

Mr Wilfred Starling asked Angelica to read her portrait to the class first, to get it over with. As he had expected and as Jamie Nutbeam had hoped, Angelica's aunt sounded anything but wonderfully interesting. She had always lived in the same street, her favourite colour was deep purple and she grew African violets on the bathroom shelf, but that was about all.

Many of the other portraits weren't much better, although there was one uncle who had fallen into Lake Burley Griffin and been rescued by a passing Member of Parliament. Someone else's aunt had competed in a penny-farthing bicycle race in Northern Tasmania, only to capsize and sprain both her knees; and there was a great-uncle who had been present at the opening of the Sydney Harbour Bridge in 1932, but couldn't remember it at all as he'd been asleep in his pram at the time.

Mr Starling saved Jamie's portrait until last, hoping for the best. Jamie cleared his throat nervously and began:

'I have never met Aunt Millicent and no one in my family knows her very well, as she hasn't been in Australia for a long time. This is because Aunt Millicent is an explorer ...'

Mr Wilfred Starling had been hoping for a bright spot in

his day, and Aunt Millicent Nutbeam was it. He smiled happily when Jamie explained how Millicent had gained her early training as an explorer by regularly running away from home. He sighed with pleasure as Jamie described the swampy region of Lake Chad, where Millicent was searching through the mud and papyrus for the northern border of the Cameroons. He positively beamed when he heard that Grandma Nutbeam was knitting explorer's socks for her daughter.

The rest of the class sat spellbound as Jamie read on, except for Angelica Tonks, whose scowl grew darker by the minute. Jamie had barely finished his portrait when her hand was waving furiously.

Mr Starling's beam faded. 'What *is* it, Angelica?'

'I don't believe it. Women don't go exploring! I think Jamie's made it all up! He's a cheat!'

Mr Starling's stomach lurched, but before he had time to say anything the other girls in the class rose up in a passion and rounded on Angelica.

'Who *says* women don't go exploring?'

'Women can do anything they want to these days, Angelica Tonks! Don't you know that?'

'*I'd* really like to be an explorer or something – maybe a test-pilot.'

'Well, *I'd* like to be a diver and explore the ocean floor and have a good look at the *Titanic*.'

'What does your aunt wear when she's at work?'

'What colour are her new socks?'

The boys began to join in.

'Can your aunt really use a machete?'

'How many languages can she speak?'

'Does she always carry a gun? I bet she's a crack shot!'

'How does a theodolite work?'

The clamour was so great that hardly anyone heard the bell. Angelica Tonks heard it and vanished in a sulk. Mr

Starling heard it and happily gathered up his books. He gave Jamie a secret wink as he left the room.

The end of the assignment was not the end of Aunt Millicent. At school, the careers teacher ran some special sessions on 'Challenging Occupations for Women' after he had been stormed by the girls from Jamie's class for information about becoming test-pilots, mobile-crane drivers, buffalo hunters and ocean-floor mappers. The Science teacher was asked to explain the workings of a theodolite to the class.

At home, Aunt Millicent settled happily into the Nutbeam family, who all followed her adventures with great interest. Dr Nutbeam brought home library books about the Cameroons and Central Africa. Jamie roared his way through one called *The Bafut Beagles*. Mrs Nutbeam rummaged through an old storeroom at the curio shop and began to collect exotic objects. She brought home a brace of hunting spears from Kenya, which she hung on the family-room wall.

'Just the sort of souvenir Millicent could have sent us,' she explained. 'See – those marks on the blades are very probably dried bloodstains.'

Another time she unwrapped a stuffed mongoose, announcing that Auntie had sent this from India on one of her earlier trips.

Jamie and Nerissa stroked it. 'What a funny animal,' said Nerissa. 'Like a weasel.'

Grandma was knitting her way down the second sock leg. 'That funny animal is a very brave creature,' she admonished, tapping the mongoose with her knitting needle. 'I'll always remember Kipling's story of Rikki-Tikki-Tavi and how he fought that dreadful king cobra. Brrr!'

'Who won?' asked Jamie.

'You could read it yourself and find out, young man,' said Grandma, starting to knit a new row. 'I expect Millicent has met a few cobras in her time.'

Nerissa had splendid dreams nearly every night. Aunt Millicent strode through most of them, wielding her machete or shouldering her theodolite. Sometimes Nerissa found herself wading through swirling rivers or swinging on jungle vines like a gibbon. Jamie was often there, too, or some of her school friends, or Grandma followed by a mongoose on a lead. Once, Mrs Nutbeam speared a giant toad, which exploded and woke Nerissa up. In another dream, Nerissa's father was polishing the fangs of a grinning crocodile, which lay back in the dentist's chair with its long tail tucked neatly under the steriliser. It looked slightly like Mrs Tonks.

Mrs Nutbeam brought home still more curios: a bamboo flute and a small tom-tom which Jamie and Nerissa soon learnt to play. Mysterious drumbeats and thin flutey tunes drifted along the street from the Nutbeams' house. School friends came to beat the tom-tom and to stroke the mongoose and to see how the explorer's socks were growing.

'Will you be sending them off soon, to the Cameroons?' they asked Grandma, who was turning the heel of the second sock.

'I think I'll make another pair, perhaps even three pairs,' replied Grandma. 'I might just as well send a large parcel as a small one.'

'Yes, and then Aunt Millie will have spare pairs of socks she can wash,' said Nerissa. 'Socks must get very smelly near the equator.'

Word of Millicent Nutbeam, intrepid explorer, began to spread through the town. Children told their families about the spears, the tom-tom, the mongoose and the khaki socks. Not every small town could claim to be connected to a famous international explorer – it was exciting news.

Angelica Tonks, however, told her mother that she didn't believe Jamie's aunt was an explorer at all. 'I bet he just invented that to make his aunt seem more interesting than all the rest,' she scoffed.

Mrs Tonks sniffed a good deal and then decided it was time to have a dental check-up. 'I'll get to the bottom of that Millicent Nutbeam, you mark my words,' she told Angelica, as she telephoned Dr Nutbeam's surgery for an appointment.

'Well, well – good morning Mrs Tonks,' said Dr Nutbeam, a few days later. 'We haven't seen you for a while! Just lie right back in the chair please, and relax!'

Mrs Tonks lay back, but she didn't relax one bit. Her eyes were sharp and suspicious. 'Good morning, Dr Nutbeam. How is the family?' she enquired. 'And how is your sister?'

Dr Nutbeam pulled on his rubber gloves. 'My sister? Which one? ... Er, probe, please nurse.'

Before he could say 'Open wide', Mrs Tonks snapped, 'Your sister the so-called explorer. Huh! The one in the Cameroons.'

'Ah, *that* sister. You mean Millicent ... now, just open wider and turn this way a little. Yes, our Millie, she does work so hard ... oops, there's a beaut cavity! A real crater!' He crammed six plugs of cotton wool around Mrs Tonks's gums. 'My word, what a lot of saliva! We'll have some suction please nurse, and just wipe that dribble from the patient's chin.' He continued to poke and scrape Mrs Tonks's molars, none too gently. 'Ah, here's another trouble spot. Mm ... have you ever been to the Cameroons, Mrs Tonks?'

Mrs Tonks's eyes glared. She tried to shake her head, but could only gurgle, 'Arggg ...'

'No, I didn't think you had. Such a fascinating place!' Dr Nutbeam turned on the squealing high-speed drill and bored into her decaying tooth, spraying water all over her chin.

When he had told his family about this encounter with Mrs Tonks, his wife complained, 'It's all very well for you. *You* can just cram people's mouths full of wadding and metal contraptions and suction tubes if they start asking awkward questions, but what am I supposed to do?'

71

The truth was that increasing numbers of townsfolk were calling at the antique shop where Mrs Nutbeam worked. They were eager to know more about Millicent Nutbeam and her adventurous life. They felt proud of her.

'It's getting quite tricky,' Mrs Nutbeam explained. 'People are asking to see photos of Millicent and wanting us to talk at the elderly citizens' club about her. This aunt is becoming an embarrassment. I wish people weren't so curious. Sometimes I don't know what to say!'

Grandma found herself on slippery ground, too, when she met the postman at the gate.

'Morning,' he said, sorting through his mailbag. 'You must be Jamie's grandmother, then.'

'Yes, I am,' Grandma replied, rather surprised.

'Mother of the explorer, eh?'

'Gracious!' exclaimed Grandma. 'Fancy you knowing about that!'

'Oh, my girl Julie has told us all about it. She's in Jamie's class at school. Funny thing – Julie's gone round the twist since she heard about all that exploring business. Says she wants to buy a camel and ride it round Australia, and one of her friends is going to apply for a job on an oil rig. I ask you!'

'Well, that's nice,' said Grandma, soothingly. 'Girls are so enterprising these days.'

'Huh! Mad, I call it.' The postman held out a bundle of letters. 'Here you are. Now, that's *another* funny thing – the Nutbeams don't get much foreign mail, come to think of it. You'd think the explorer would write to them more often, her being in the travelling line.'

Grandma breathed deeply. 'Oh, it's not easy, you know, writing letters when you're exploring. For one thing, there's never a decent light in the tent at night – and besides, there's hardly ever a post office to hand when you need it.' She glanced through the letters. 'Goodness! There's one from South America ... Peru.'

'That's what made me wonder. Is it from her?' asked the postman, eagerly.

'Her? Ah . . . Millicent. I don't know. It's for Dr Nutbeam, my son, and it's typed. Anyway, as far as we know, Millicent is still in the Cameroons, although we've not had word for some time.'

'She could have moved on, couldn't she?' suggested the postman, 'Peru, eh? Oh well, I'd better move on, too. G'day to you!'

At school, Julie the postman's daughter said to Jamie, 'Why has your auntie gone to South America? What's she exploring now?'

'Who said she's gone to South America?' demanded Jamie. He felt he was losing control of Aunt Millicent.

'My dad said there was a letter from her in Peru,' replied Julie.

'Well, no one told *me*,' growled Jamie.

At home he announced, 'Julie is telling everybody that our Aunt Millicent is in Peru! What's she talking about? What's happening?'

Grandma stopped knitting. 'Julie. Is that the name of the postman's girl?'

'Yes – her dad said there was a letter for us from Auntie in Peru, or somewhere mad.'

'Oh, I remember – he asked me about it,' said Grandma.

'Well . . . what did you *say*?' wailed Jamie.

'I just said I didn't know who the letter was from and that I thought Millicent was still in the Cameroons, but that we hadn't heard for a while where she was. That's all.'

'The letter from Peru,' chuckled Dr Nutbeam, 'is about the World Dental Conference on plaque, which is being held next year in Lima. It has nothing to do with Millicent.'

'Well of *course* it hasn't,' spluttered Jamie. 'She doesn't exist!'

'But Jamie, in a funny sort of way she *does* exist,' said Mrs Nutbeam.

His father grinned. 'My sister is quite a girl! She's begun to live a life of her own!'

'That's the trouble,' said Jamie. 'She seems to be doing things we don't know about.'

While they were talking, the telephone rang. Dr Nutbeam was no longer grinning when he came back from answering it. 'That was Frank Figgis from the local paper.'

'Frank, the editor?' asked Mrs Nutbeam. 'What did he want?'

'He wants to do a full-page feature on our Millicent,' groaned her husband. 'He's heard that she's about to set out on a climbing expedition in the Andes! Up some peak that has never yet been conquered!'

'What nonsense!' snapped Grandma. 'She's too old for that sort of thing.'

'It's just a rumour!' shouted Jamie. 'Who said she's going to the Andes? *I* didn't say she was going there. She's still in the Cameroons!'

'Calm down, dear,' said his mother, 'and let's hear what Dad said to Frank Figgis.'

Dr Nutbeam was rubbing his head. 'I stalled for time – I said we'd not heard she was in the Andes, but that we'd make enquiries and let him know. Whatever happens, Millicent mustn't get into print. We'll all be up on a charge of false pretences or something!'

Jamie snorted. 'Well, if she's climbing an Ande, it might be best if she fell off and was never seen again.'

Nerissa shrieked, '*No*! She mustn't – she's our only aunt and we've only just got her!'

Mrs Nutbeam sighed. 'Listen, Jamie, perhaps the time has come to own up that Aunt Millicent is not real.'

'We can't do that!' wailed Jamie. 'Everyone would think we're loony . . . and that Grandma's absolutely bonkers, knitting socks for an aunt who isn't there. And what about the mongoose? Anyway, I *can't* let Honky Tonks find out now – she'd never stop crowing and she'd be more awful than ever.'

Jamie decided to lay the whole problem of Aunt Millicent Nutbeam before Mr Starling, right up to her unexpected expedition to the Andes and Mr Figgis's plan to write a full page feature about her for the local paper. He finished by saying, 'I think I might have to kill her off.'

'That'd be a shame,' sighed Mr Starling. 'She's quite a lady, your aunt!'

'It would be pretty easy to get rid of her,' Jamie went on. 'In her sort of job she could sink into a quicksand, or be trampled by a herd of elephants, or something.'

Mr Starling shook his head violently. 'No, no – it would only make things worse if she died a bloodcurdling death like that. No one would be likely to forget her if she was squashed flat by a stampeding elephant. She'd become more interesting than ever!'

'Well, she could die of something boring, like pneumonia,' said Jamie. 'Or ... will I have to own up that she isn't real?'

'Do you want to own up?'

'Not really. I'd feel stupid, and I specially don't want Angelica Tonks to know I invented an aunt.'

Mr Starling quite understood. 'I see! Anyway, a lot of people would be sad to discover that Millicent Nutbeam was a hoax. The girls in your class, for example – she means a lot to them.'

'What'll I do then?'

'If you want people to lose interest in her, you'll just have to make her less interesting. I think she should retire from exploring, for a start.'

'Aw, gee!' Jamie felt very disappointed. 'I suppose so. I'll see what they think at home.'

*   *   *

'What he means,' said Dr Nutbeam, when Jamie had repeated Mr Starling's advice, 'is that it's time my dear sister Millicent settled down.'

'I quite agree with that,' remarked Grandma, who was up to the sixth sock foot. 'She's not as young as she was, and it's high time she had some normal home life. I think she should get married, even though she's getting on a bit. Perhaps to a widower.'

'That sounds terribly boring,' yawned Nerissa.

'Well, that's what we need,' said Jamie, 'something terribly boring to make people lose interest.'

Grandma sniffed. 'In my day it would have been called a happy ending.'

'Well, I suppose it's a happier ending than being squashed by an elephant,' conceded Jamie.

'How about marrying her to a retired accountant who used to work for a cardboard box company?' suggested his father. 'That sounds pretty dull.'

'Good heavens, it's all rather sudden!' said Mrs Nutbeam. 'Last time we heard of her she was climbing the Andes!'

'No, she *wasn't*.' At last Jamie felt he had hold of Aunt Millicent again. 'That South American stuff was just a rumour. The postman started it because of the letter from Peru, and then the story just grew!'

Dr Nutbeam nodded. 'Stories seem to have a habit of doing that, and so do rumours! But we can easily squash this one about the Andes. I'll just explain about the World Dental Conference on plaque. I even have the letter to prove it.'

Dr Nutbeam called Frank Figgis on the phone. He explained about the letter from Peru and about the ridiculous rumour which the postman had started. 'In your profession, Frank,' he added sternly, 'you should be much more careful than to listen to baseless rumour. It could get you into all sorts of trouble! In any case, Millicent is giving up exploring to marry a retired accountant. She's had enough.'

Frank Figgis was fast losing interest. 'I see – well, some-time when she's in Australia, we could do an interview about her former life . . . maybe.'

'Maybe, although she has no immediate plans to return here. I believe she and her husband are going to settle down in England – somewhere on the seafront, like Bognor.'

Jamie passed on the same information to his classmates. The girls were shocked.

'She's what?'

'Getting married to an *accountant*?'

'She can't be!'

'How boring for her!'

'Where in the world is Bognor? Is there really such a place?'

Angelica Tonks smiled like a smug pussycat. 'See! Your Aunt Millicent is just like any other old aunt, after all!'

Jamie caught Mr Starling's eye. It winked.

Aunt Millicent Nutbeam retired, not to Bognor but to live quietly with her family. Nerissa still had wonderful dreams. Dr Nutbeam still brought home books about far-off places. The blood-stained spears remained on the wall and the mongoose on the shelf. Jamie and Nerissa still played the tom-tom and the bamboo flute.

Grandma Nutbeam's holiday came to an end and she packed up to return home. She left a parcel for Jamie. When he opened it, he found three pairs of khaki socks with dark blue stripes, and a card which said:

Dear Jamie,

Aunt Millicent won't have any use for these now that she has settled down, so you might as well have them for school camps. Isn't it lucky that they are just your size!

With love from Grandma.

CASTLE HAWKSMERE
Allan Baillie

Gary stopped before the old tree and *knew* something was wrong. The fir was wrestling with the wind, wide branches scything the air, the trunk creaking like a massive wooden door, the crown scratching arcs across the sky. Watch the buffeted foliage, now green, now black, and the tree was falling.

But it was always that way on days like this. Optical illusion. No, there was something else. He just could not put his finger on it.

Gary shrugged and began to climb.

Goblins. Now you're thinking they're real.

He could feel the smooth bark under his fingers as he moved, rough bark worn by years of constant climbing –

always climbing the same way. He could climb this tree blindfolded, wind or no wind.

He closed his eyes and caught a knobbed branch. He locked his legs on a fork, reached up and pulled himself against the trunk. And felt the tree groan. He opened his eyes and watched the light dancing over the heavy branches. The tree was alive.

Oh yes. Course it isn't a tree, is it? Hasn't been a tree for – maybe three years.

Gary climbed on. Slower and with his eyes open. Everything about him was moving.

Four years. Then it was a forest full of headhunters ...

He straddled a thick branch and patted it almost affectionately.

And this is where the Alien got you. The Alien got everybody – Clive climbs like a monkey. Bit of trouble stopping Clive being the Alien *all* the time. But the tree was a great space ore freighter.

Gary kicked from the branch and his hands found a wooden pulley tied to a fork with a rope – frayed to nothing – dangling.

Woody's Station. Woody would pull things up from the ground and send them all the way to the castle. It hadn't been used for a while.

Gary moved steadily up until the trunk swayed in his arms, the branches snatched at him and he could see the castle.

This is where we fight dragons, he thought. Or used to.

He could remember Cas sitting on the split branch like an old crow, telling them all what they should be seeing. Not up at the shifting square of the castle floor and the foliage, the trembling trunk and the sky. No, you are looking across a misty gorge at a splintered crag and a cloud of great black birds. The gorge is bottomless and filled with dragons, trolls, gorgons, all manner of unspeakable creatures, but on the splintered crag there is an embattled tower of pure emerald.

The last outpost of the Golden Kingdom. Castle Hawksmere. You could see it, even now.

Gary scrambled the last metres to the castle, poked his head through the entrance hole in the floor and was almost kicked. Woody was running about with rope in his hands.

'Watch it!' Gary scuttled to one side.

'Sorry, sorry.' Woody was throwing loops around the old dressing table, the castle's treasury, and tying it to the trunk. He was not even glancing at Gary. 'C'mon, give us a hand before it all gets blown away.'

Gary reeled to his feet as the floorboards rippled and David's shield toppled from its special hollow in the tree. He caught it, thrust it back into the hollow and Woody slapped the rope across the trunk to keep it there. They tied down the banquet cupboard (almost empty now), the armoury (a broken spear and the silver sword he'd made), and the scorched-edge charter written by Clive. Woody wanted to tie down the lurching walls but there was no more rope, so they sat on the floor and panted at each other.

'That was close,' said Woody.

'The dragons nearly got us,' said Gary, and jumped as two sliding boards pinched him.

'Where is she, anyway? She should be up here, helping. It's her castle.'

'It's *our* castle. We built it.' Gary stretched across to protect his sword from the rope. The carving had taken him a month, the silver paint cost him three weeks' pocket-money.

'It was her idea.'

'Well, it always is.'

The two boys looked at each other. Woody thumbed a piece of bark between his knees. Gary looked at the low walls around him, the bucking canvas above him. There was nothing to say.

But Gary stopped, went back to the branch that supported the canvas roof and remembered a little.

Four boys, hiding in their Secret Spot on the top of the old fir tree, plotting, and suddenly a skinny girl in braces and freckles is dangling upside-down among them. Trailing long black hair over Clive's face and giggling when he screams. Dave doesn't want her round, threatens to throw her from his tree. She says she'll tell everybody about the Secret Spot. She is accepted with a great deal of muttering – until she produces her first idea.

'We had ideas before,' Woody said slowly.

Gary blinked at him.

'Well, we did. No worries.'

'Sure, what? Spy on everybody that comes into the bush, be a tribe of monkeys . . .'

'That was fun. Sort of.'

'It still itches.'

'And Tarzan's house.'

'That was okay. The headhunters bit was better than some, but there was no house. Just a plank.'

Woody reached back and tapped at the wooden skeleton that held the floorboards. 'This plank.'

'Yeah. We've done a lot since . . .'

The tree suddenly shook and a noisy running battle surged up the trunk. Clive and David burst through the hole together and fell apart on the floor.

'Who won? C'mon, who won?' David shouted. A torn flap of his yellow footy jumper hung from his shoulder.

'Dunno. Wasn't watching.' Woody shrugged and pulled at one of the ropes.

'What are you doing?' Clive stared at the ropes around him.

'That's a wild wind, eh? Just feel it, Clive.' Dave took his hand off the trunk and stood, feet spread wide on the rippling boards.

Clive caught at a flapping rope end and looked nervous. 'Yeah. What do we do now, Dave?'

'Oh, I dunno.' Dave watched the tossing sea of tree tops around him. 'What about converting the castle into a pirate ship? Or a submarine ...'

'I could be a kraken.' Since the Alien Clive had become an expert on monsters.

Woody glanced at Gary. 'We've done all that before.'

'Yeah, well.' Dave sat on the treasury.

Gary kicked at a board and remembered the day Cas became a part of them. A wind like this, but with a little whirling rain; the floor moving like this, but it was only a single plank. The four of them, but just a little smaller, a little wilder – and Cas. Clive was moaning about the rain and why didn't we go home. Rain? said Cas, not just rain, a storm, a great storm! A typhoon! Look at the waves out there! We're on a sailing ship with two masts gone and what can we do?

Just sail the tree for a month, while the plank becomes a floor and the sinking sailors become pirates with a flag. Woody gets his station going, and the ship is an atomic submarine, with walls and a torpedo. A canvas roof and it is a space freighter with the Alien on board. Finally, Castle Hawksmere with shield, silver sword and a band of knights battling the dark forces from the bottomless gorge.

'The wind is dropping,' said Clive, trying to appear disappointed but carrying relief in his eyes.

Gary looked at the others and there was still something wrong.

'Anyway, where is she?' Woody said.

'She's coming,' Dave said with a shrug.

'You've seen her?' Gary said, sharply.

'Down the street.'

'She looks different,' Clive said.

'Shut up, Clive.' Dave tapped a low branch with his foot. 'We ought to go out on an adventure.'

'A mission!'

'Yeah. A mission. When did we do that last, hey?'

Gary had to think. 'Two months – five months ago?'

'Dehaunting that house.' Clive began to beam.

'We could do that again.'

'We can do better than that . . .' Gary said.

'Here she comes,' said Woody. 'I think.'

A flicker of pink moving down the bush track far below. Pink?

Clive talked of the haunted house while he waited. House? It was no more than a chimney in a burnt-out shell. But Cas declared it haunted, so ghosts and demons were zapped for one long night, and Clive said he saw a white mist rising in the blackened fireplace.

'Hi, guys.'

Gary stared at the girl half-way through the entrance hole and his shoulders sagged. This was Cas, but not the Cas he had known. That Cas wore her hair long, pulled back by an elastic band; she carried mud on her face like war-paint; she dressed in tattered jeans, T-shirt and runners. *This* Cas wore her hair short and swept to the right of her head; she dressed in a pink shirt, a grey skirt and grey flat shoes; she wore something on her lips. She was *old*.

But Clive couldn't see it. 'Hi Cas. What're we going to do today? Wipe the trolls?'

Cas climbed into the castle, carefully to keep her skirt clean. 'I dunno, Clive. What do you think?' But she wasn't listening for an answer.

'What's with the flash threads, Cas?'

'Just felt like it, Dave.' She reached for the carved and painted shield, swords behind a plumed helmet, and ran her hand slowly over it.

'Me masterpiece, hey?'

She nodded. 'Never saw just how good it was . . .' She replaced the shield, hefted Gary's silver sword, touched Clive's ancient charter and stopped.

'What's wrong, Cas?' Gary said softly.

She shook her head. 'Just a minute,' she said in a faint voice.

Woody frowned at Gary and moved toward Cas. 'C'mon. We're all mates here.'

Gary saw Cas's eyes shimmering, wondered, and waited.

'Aren't we?' Woody glared about him. Clive, David, Gary nodded and watched her face.

'Oh hell.' Cas was trying to sound bright. 'It's nothing. Much.'

'All right. We'll fix it,' said David. 'Castle Hawksmere can fix anything.'

Cas shook her head. 'It's a lot of little things.'

She ran her thumb over the blade of the silver sword.

'Mum and Dad are fighting again. Most days. Dad keeps asking me whether I am aiming for university, suddenly exams mean what you're going to do for the rest of your life. I even have to train to play tennis now. I have to train to do *everything* now. I have to wear things, and Becky Thomas is going to be a mum in four months and I used to play basketball with her . . .'

Cas looked around at us. 'I'm not making much sense, hey?'

David shrugged.

Cas closed the book and stood up. 'What I mean is it's all changing now. So fast . . . Does anyone understand me.'

Gary spoke very softly. 'You don't want to come to the castle any more.'

Cas nodded once. 'I guess I can't. Any more.'

She climbed awkwardly into the hole and tossed the silver sword of Castle Hawksmere to Gary. Gary missed it, saw it fall to the floor and split into two clumsy pieces of painted wood. A broken toy.

'Sorry, guys.' She tried to say something else, shook her head.

And was gone.

YOU CAN'T KEEP A UNICORN
Patricia Wrightson

When I first saw Samantha she was four weeks old, one of ten pups like furry caterpillars; pearl-coloured, with assorted black patches and stringy tails. They were piled up in a sort of pyramid between their mother's front legs, gazing out with sleepy, wondering eyes. From our car Pandy stared suspiciously back. She was Peter's pup, already five months old; big and strong and fast for her age, shiny-black with a spotted white ruff like a Wyandotte rooster's. A rewarding pup, but I needed a blue heeler of my own.

I had first choice of this ten – or were there only nine? Then I heard a tiny, fierce bark: the tenth was by itself, backed up against the wall of the shed and barking defiantly. It looked and sounded ridiculous.

'Perhaps that one,' I suggested.

'It's the smallest,' they warned me kindly, and showed me another four or five.

It was hard to choose when they were such babies and all so much alike. I nursed a few; they were as soft as kittens and as solemn as clowns, and they wore their black patches like clowns, mostly over one or both eyes. But their pearly colour and black patches would change. The smallest, the one against the wall, had only black ears. It wobbled forward, barked its tiny bark and sat down heavily on the grass. I bent to pick it up.

It was sitting on a bee arched ready to sting. I picked up the puppy, and the bee stung me instead. Oh, well; if you're going to own a very small puppy it seems only right to prevent it from being stung. 'This one,' I said, pulling out the sting from my hand.

'What's her name?' the owners asked, for the puppy was to stay a few more weeks with them and its mother.

Blue heeler dogs are always called Blue, a sound reason for choosing something else. Some good, plain name for a nice, sensible country girl. 'Debbie, perhaps?'

Debbie! Whatever else Samantha might be she was never a nice, sensible country girl. We mostly called her Sam.

When we went to fetch her home, she was seven weeks old and about the size of your shoe. Her mother ran barking beside the car to see her off, not angry but sounding like any other mother: 'Be sure to keep your nest clean and wash around your tail!' Pandy's eyes flared with excitement. Sam tried not to see her, licked my hand politely and set about finding things to chew. She had turned the proper silver-grey colour, with the proper white mark between her black ears, and a large black patch over each eye.

At home we put her in the shade-house, for she was not house-trained and too small to play with Pandy. The shade-house had no door, but Peter made a barrier of wire-netting instead. The two pups sniffed each other through the netting. In five minutes the big one was inside and the little one outside the shade-house.

Peter made the barrier twice as high.

Sam stood on her hind legs, front feet on the netting, and set up a storm of yelping. Pandy, frowning with worry, lay close against the netting on the outside. Sam worked up the scale from reason to protest, to fury, and at last to pleading. At this point she broke into words, clearly and beautifully pronounced: 'Chihuahua, chihuahua, woe! Woe!'

I had the washing to do. I gave her an old coat to lie on, a dish of water and another of puppy-food, a newspaper to tear up and a bone to play with. On my way to the clothesline I peeped at her. She was asleep on the newspaper, but at once woke and leapt to the wire-netting, yelping to be taken out, clinging with sharp little claws to my wrist while I stroked her. When I took the clothes-basket inside, she broke again into sobs and howls.

'Chihuahua, chihuahua, woe! Woe!'

At last it was time for afternoon walks. Pandy needed a good, energetic walk up to the bush, with some time on the lead, some time racing at speed along tracks mown in the long grass, and some more time learning not to chase wallabies. Samantha needed to play on the short grass near the house. When Peter and Pandy had gone, I took her a little way down the hill on a small cat's lead. She fought it fiercely.

When I sat on the grass she made a joyful attack on my wrists and ankles, and climbed up to chew my ears. It was the only play she knew, but her little teeth and claws were like needles. It hurt less if I found a stick for her to attack, and that began her career as an expert with sticks.

Then she invented a game: Sam's Game, which we played on many walks. She would steal away up the hill and hide in the grass, full of wickedness and cunning. When I could stop laughing I would call, 'Oh dear, where *has* that puppy gone?' and Samantha would come hurtling like a demon down the hill and leap on me.

That was pretty painful until I learnt to appeal to her better nature. 'Oh dear, oh dear,' I would quaver in terror, 'where is that fierce, ferocious puppy? I'm so frightened of that puppy! Where is it?' Sam would come pelting down as hard as ever, but only to race around me in mad circles.

After her walk she was fed and put snugly to bed inside a cardboard carton, in the sunroom that is also my office. With Samantha, nothing was ever easy: putting her to bed meant holding her down while she yelped and fought, and at last finding an old net curtain to tie over the carton and keep her in. Finally, I closed the door and went away.

'Chihuahua, chihuahua, woe! Woe!'

Later I found her asleep on the outside of the carton, hanging suspended in a bulge of net. I took her for a toilet-walk and snuggled her down again, tying the curtain tighter. At two a.m. I was wakened by loud calls from the sunroom, and the booming and crashing of the door in its frame. Samantha was free of the curtain, pounding on the door to ask for another toilet-walk. She grew very fond of that curtain. Sometimes she slept on it and sometimes she wore it around the place: Sam's Veil.

During the day she stayed in my office while I worked – as Pandy stayed in Peter's office with him. Samantha would play with her ball or a shoe until she was sleepy, then come bird-twittering round my ankles to be nursed. When she had fallen asleep on my knee, under the edge of the desk, I would settle her on a cushion in the sun.

There were early morning as well as evening walks. Pandy resented these separate walks, for the two pups were eager to be friends. Pandy would come hurrying home from the bush and track to and fro near the house, determined to know where Samantha and I had been, tracing our scent along the hill in the mown grass.

It was because of that mown grass that I failed to find Samantha's tick. I searched her every day, but not very carefully; we had never had ticks near the house, and I was really only teaching her to lie still and be patient. When she collapsed one morning, and I found a big tick in the deep fur under her neck, I was frightened. She was still so small.

We rushed with her into town to the vet. She spent a day and a night in the clinic, being given serum by drip. When we went to bring her home she was very wobbly, from drugs and from tick-paralysis; but she yapped and wriggled with joy while she tried to clamber all over us.

I was given some very serious advice: Samantha must not get excited; she must not on any account have another tick this year; for a few days must have only tiny amounts of food and water, or the paralysis might cause her to choke. Anxiously we took her home to her cardboard carton bed.

We already knew Samantha had only two states: she was asleep or she was excited. I carried her down the front steps for a toilet-walk, balanced her briefly on a garden bed, and carried her back inside – and she had another tick. This time I found and removed it at once. About food and water she was just as uncompromising.

I gave her the tiny spoonfuls the vet had advised. In pathetic yelps she begged me to have a heart, she'd had nothing for two days, she was starving! I gave her another spoonful and went away, firmly closing the office door. At once it began to bounce and rattle and boom: paralysed or not, Samantha was pounding on it. 'Food! Food!' she yelled.

It was hard to resist. I gave her slightly more, and oftener. Samantha wobbled weakly out to the kitchen and sat by the refrigerator; she was going to stay there till she died. I gave her a *very small* meal and shut her in the office again. 'Food!

Food!' yelled Samantha, pounding on the door. It was a choice between tiny spoonfuls and not getting excited. On the second day I gave in and fed her with small meals very often. Samantha collected another tick at the back door and set about getting well.

In a week she was full of life and cheerful wickedness. She had even grown to the size of a cat. Everyone agreed that she would never be a big dog; she had such a light, fine frame. Samantha was content to make use of what she had and began to play wild games with Pandy.

Pandy, too, had grown. She was long and lithe with strong legs, a fast and powerful runner. Though Sam was fast for her size she had no chance of keeping up, and she learnt to dodge when Pandy, carried away by excitement, ran straight at her. She had no chance, either, in the tussles and tumbles and pretended fights, except through Pandy's goodwill.

'Gently, Pandy, gently! She's only little!'

And Pandy would shift her grip or her weight and look up anxiously, saying, 'Is this gentle?' Or she would lie on her back, pretending to be helpless, letting Sam throttle her.

But if Sam was lighter, and slower in speed, she was quicker in other ways and she never gave in. She learnt to stroll innocently near, admiring the view, and then to make a quick, nipping dart at Pandy's paw or tail and be away while Pandy was still saying, 'Ouch!' She learnt that, while anyone can stand on three legs, no ordinary dog can stand on two; she would run under Pandy with a quick nip to right and left so that Pandy, instinctively lifting two bitten feet, fell down. She learnt about centrifugal force, and used it in the house where Pandy's big claws could not grip.

Big bodies, travelling round corners at speed, swing wider than small bodies. Running on the grass, Pandy could control this swing by gripping with her claws in the soft soil. On a hard floor it was different.

Samantha, with a cunning dart, seized the ball or the old

shoe and fled: right through one door, left through the next, sharp right round the big green chair and again under the coffee-table, left through the office door, right under my work-table and back by the same twisting route. Big Pandy came after her, one leap behind but scrabbling for traction on every corner. Little Samantha, stretched to a gallop, ears flat and eyes full of glee, could just manage to stay in front till she dropped the ball or ran out of breath.

This was her good time. I never knew anything so alive as Sam; she was in love with life and people. Sometimes she talked to you in a companionable way: not growling or barking but making a deep, vibrating noise like a wildebeest. If you stepped outside to pick a little parsley, she welcomed you back as if you had been away for a week. Yet she had a host of enemies and subdued them gleefully every day: the brush from the dustpan, the vacuum cleaner when it came to life, the spade, the shovel, the rake. As often as Peter propped a tool against the shed, Samantha leapt on it and battled it to the ground.

She fought with sticks on her walks, and leapt after them into the air, and twisted in mid-air to catch them, until she seemed to fly like a bird. She taught Pandy to play with sticks; for now we followed Peter and Pandy on walks, till they turned back to meet us and we all came home together – Pandy and Samantha carrying a stick between them, heads high, trotting together like a pair of well-bred horses.

'Little unicorn,' I said to Samantha one day.

Peter objected. 'Unicorn? She hasn't got a horn.'

'Of course not – she rammed it into a tree. But you can see the white patch between her ears where it used to be.'

All the same, I was surprised. I hadn't meant to call Sam a unicorn, it just came out. Both dogs had beautiful horse gaits, high-stepping, contained, with heads lifted; and of course a unicorn is like a horse. But no one would call Pandy a unicorn, though she had an elfish, slippery sense of fun.

Why should I call Samantha a unicorn?

Yet the name stuck, and Peter used it too. Unicorns are wild and fierce and loving; they are gallant and free and can only be captured by gentleness. That was Sam: a very little unicorn with black eye-patches and a shattered horn. And I was sure that a unicorn's call would be deep and vibrating, like a wildebeest's.

Summer began, and Pandy took Sam swimming in the waterhole down on the flat. Two or three times a day they would come back grinning happily, Pandy wet to the elbows and Sam with her ears full of water-weed. We took them down to the Broadwater, to show them a real waterhole.

It stretched away flat and shining, five kilometres to the distant shore, a daunting sight. Pandy had seen it when she was smaller: once when she backed away cautiously, once when she paddled on the edge. She paddled again now, but Samantha stared with round eyes and walked solemnly into the water.

In a few paces she was out of her depth, still going, her eyes fixed on us in a questioning way. 'Is this right? I'm swimming, aren't I? How do I stop?' We applauded and gave her a knee to climb; and then we saw Pandy.

Pandy was outraged, indignant. 'Little show-off! *I* showed her the waterhole! Who does she think she is?' When Sam had struggled out, Pandy knocked her over two or three times and went and sat on the upturned boat. After a little sulking, she stole quietly away into the water and swam, too.

Christmas came, and each of our pups had a tough plastic animal that whistled when you squeezed it. They held these in their mouths, a rooster-tail sticking out here and a rabbit-head there, and raced through the house chewing gently: *whee! whee!* It was a shrill sort of Christmas.

Sam was six months old when a cloud began to hang over her. Between wild, fierce struggles with Pandy, bird-flights after a stick, battles with the rake and joyous races through the house, she was sometimes quiet and strained. Sometimes she limped, or cried when I lifted her. I thought that in some crazy leap she might have strained her back. But the vet's treatment for a strained back didn't seem to help, and at last I asked for an X-ray.

It took most of a day, for dogs are not good at lying still in the right positions for X-rays; they need an anaesthetic. We left Samantha at the clinic and, while we waited, drove to the next town to do some business. Hours later we returned; you could hear Sam's impatient yells from the street outside the clinic.

'You got back to town ten minutes ago' said the nurse in a resigned way. 'She heard you.'

Samantha did not have a strained back. The X-rays showed a broken bone in her spine, and two others damaged.

No one knew what accident had happened – or how she had gone on playing in spite of the pain. To fix it she would need an operation on her spine, and then to stay quiet and still in a cage for six weeks. I didn't worry about the operation: it would be done by a good surgeon who would care for her till she was safe. But to cage a unicorn . . .

'It will be much worse than for most dogs,' Peter and I agreed with sinking hearts. 'But then, she has more life than most dogs, to make it worthwhile.'

We had help. Our vet's name was Kim, and she too knew the cage would be the bad part for Sam. We had the loan of one of her cages, and drugs to use in a careful plan for keeping Samantha quiet. To keep her sane, our butcher sent wonderful bones: not too big or too small, with lots of meat and gristle to keep a dog busy for a whole day; a bone for Sam every day, and some for poor, troubled Pandy. Pandy knew a vet's cage when she saw it. When ours came home she looked at it in a startled way, nosed all around it, then sat in it quietly for some time, thinking.

I don't like to remember those six weeks. Sam, drugged or

weary and hopeless in her cage, being carried into my office by day or my bedroom at night, to keep her from excitement and fretting; taking quiet, obedient toilet-walks on a lead and only sometimes making a little dart at a stick, or a leap at the rake standing against the shed; growling angrily over her bones because they were all she had; crying softly to herself until we had to take her out of the cage and comfort her. But she knew the reason was in her own back. She was a good patient, and at last the X-rays showed that the bones were healed. Sam must still take care, but she could come out of the cage.

Six weeks is a long time in the life of a puppy. How should I set her free without too much wild excitement? More drugs, perhaps; but there had been so many. In the end I put the daily bone in her cage, and just left the door open. Sam considered this while she chewed the bone, lying half in and half out of the cage. She stayed like that until Peter and Pandy had gone for their walk. Then she ventured out, carrying the bone, and walked all through the house. I don't think she saw me watching. After a while she began to run.

It wasn't a wild, excited run but very light and lively. Sam ran lightly through the house, to and fro, tossing her bone in the air and catching it.

Next day we gave the two pups a ten-minute party to celebrate. If you have any small animals to entertain (or if you want them to entertain you), the best thing is a bubble-party. It's very easy; you just dip the little wire thing into the special suds and wave it in the air, sending strings of bubbles into the breeze and letting them come down where they will.

Cats stalk them cunningly, and are startled and offended when they suddenly disappear. If you have a cat who thinks rather too much of himself, bubbles may cure him of smugness.

Birds fly in circles around them, protecting their nests but taking no foolish risks, and swagger off when the floating bubble bursts; or they hold solemn meetings round a bubble at rest on the grass, and go on arguing in a frustrated way when it vanishes. Dogs have fun, leaping and catching the bubbles, as excited as small children and enjoying the taste of suds.

Now only Pandy leapt to catch our bubbles. Sam had learnt about pain, and snapped them up eagerly as they floated down.

For a month we were all careful. Sam and Pandy were not allowed to tussle. It was hard for them, but pain is a good teacher and Pandy had learnt months ago what it meant when someone cried, 'Gently!' Sam was fierce and joyful and loving again, but now she was more careful. No one could keep her from battling with all her old enemies or attacking a stick; but the stick could be kept on the ground to avoid leaping, and the tools could be hidden or not allowed to fall. We were patient: in a year she would be strong and well, and still young enough for wicked glee.

But in a month there was more pain, more X-rays, more damage to Sam's spine. There had never been an accident; only a rare condition, known but not understood, not able to be cured. There was nothing ahead but pain, and we had to take her back to Kim for one last, kind needle.

I miss her. Often I wonder, as I always did, into what that wild, free spirit, fierce and loving, might have grown. But you can't keep a unicorn long enough to find out.

INITIATION
Christobel Mattingley

It's not always easy to get a job. Especially in a small country town. It's hard when you left school at Year Nine. It's even harder when you're Aboriginal.

Some of the fellas seemed to accept that being unemployed was a full-time job. Sitting around outside the post office. Waiting for the dole cheque. Playing cards. Watching the birds walk by. Sitting around outside the pub. Waiting for it to open. Kicking a Coke can. Flicking a pebble. Watching the tourists go by in their four-wheel drives with their caravans, or in cars with roof racks piled with camping gear, heading to the ranges.

Tinkering with a cousin's motor bike. Burning up the highway for fifty ks or more until the engine splutters and dies. Never getting near the ranges. Flagging down a motorist for petrol to get back or hitching a lift on a heavy transport.

Scuffling. Sparring. Swearing. Yesterday. Today. Tomorrow. Last week. This week. Next week. Last year. This year. Next year. Staring. Staring across to the ranges. The ranges where the old people used to live. A hundred years ago. A thousand years ago. Forty thousand years ago.

Piling into a friend's HD Holden. Roaring up the highway for fifty ks or more until the engine splutters and dies. Never getting near the ranges. Hitching a lift back home. Home to the pub.

But for Wayne Williams it wasn't enough. The emptiness of it gnawed his gut. The futility of it ferreted his mind. He wanted out.

But the ranges were out of bounds. His ancestors' hunting grounds were sheep and cattle stations now. Had been for almost 150 years since the Udnyu came with their four-footed cloven-hoofed stock, their fencing wire and their firearms. Wayne's grandfathers and father had worked for the invaders as shepherds and stationhands. But now with motor bikes and vehicles and two-way radios there were few places for stockmen on Yura lands. And the ranges had become a playground for tourists, who swarmed in seasonal plagues, like locusts, in winter, spring and summer. The Yura people were mostly fringe-dwellers now in the little townships which had sprung up to serve the pastoral properties and the tourist industry.

Wayne had been out to the ranges with his uncles. He had looked out from their peaks. He had walked the watercourses running like veins through the land which had nurtured his people since the Dreamtime began. He had listened to some of the stories.

But before he was born the elders had decided to discontinue the initiation of their young men. They feared the power of the white man's grog. Men drank it to assuage their own powerlessness and despair, and in its grip they could let slip the sacred secrets.

Wayne had a cousin who had gone south to the city. He was a strong man, not afraid to tell the Udnyu that they needed to listen and learn about the ancient culture of the land. He told Wayne of a job coming up in the city, a job that would help the Udnyu begin to understand the traditional owners of Australia. Wayne wrote his application in his best hand, posted it and waited. Waited for day after day, sitting on the roadway outside the post office, staring out at the ranges.

One day the letter came, asking Wayne to travel to the city for an interview. His ticket was enclosed. Wayne boarded the bus in his best flannelette shirt and jeans. Through the tinted window he watched the ranges curving south in rippled purple folds against the eastern sky. The bus reached the port at the head of the gulf, the biggest town Wayne knew. The ranges were receding, the sea was beginning. The bus charged on, past rolling paddocks of ripening grain, on and on towards the city, the city Wayne had never seen.

The interview was in a bigger building than Wayne had ever seen. The people poked with their questions and probed him with their eyes. They filled his ears with their words and sent him away, telling him they would write and let him know.

Wayne travelled home alone. Alone with his thoughts and impressions and wonderings. Home to the post office. Staring out at the ranges. Waiting in the October warmth for the promised letter.

When it came it said he had not got the job.

Wayne wondered what he could do. He wondered what he could do to help his people. He thought of the Udnyu city with the hurrying Udnyu people, their tall buildings and their shops, their cars and their noise. He stared out at the ranges where every scarp, every stream had its silent story, where every living thing had its place in the Dreamtime.

While he was still pondering, a second letter came. It said that the position had not been filled, and invited Wayne to re-apply. Wayne wrote out his application again in his neatest writing. He posted it and waited. Waited for a week. Waited for another week. And another.

Then the third letter came. The bus ticket fell out. He was invited to the city for another interview. He boarded the bus in his best T-shirt and jeans. Doubt dragged at his feet but hope hugged his heart. The ranges receded, the sea sparkled, the suburbs stretched in brick veneer packages bound with galvanized fences.

The interview repeated itself. Like fried onions. Rings and layers. Greasy. Circular questions and hidden agenda. Smooth words. A promise of a letter.

Wayne travelled home alone. Alone with feelings of hope and doubt and distrust. Two days staying with his cousin seeing the sights of the city in Christmas tinsel did not compensate for the feeling that he had been used.

He sat outside the post office. Waiting for the letter. Flicking at the flies. Drawing in the dust. Looking out at the ranges. Wondering about Udnyu ways. Wondering what he could do for his people.

He waited through the November heat. He waited into December. The post office became suddenly busy as people came to send cards and presents to family and friends far away, and went off clutching parcels and letters with city postmarks.

Then at last the letter Wayne was waiting for arrived. It thanked him for attending the interview. It was sorry, but the job had gone to someone else.

Wayne walked along to the pub. All the fellas were there. Scuffling. Sparring. Swearing. Waiting for the pub to open.

Waiting for the first drink. And the second. And the flagon to follow. Wayne waited with them.

The tourists were waiting too, to douse the dust in their throats and have the last drink for a hundred ks until they reached the pub in the ranges. Their vehicles were lined up outside, Range Rovers, Land Cruisers, Pajeros, Jackeroos, air-conditioned Mercedes, Volvos, Peugeots packed with gear.

They pointed their cameras at the distant ranges, fiddling with telephoto lenses. 'It'll be hot,' they commiserated with each other. 'But it will be worth it. They say the colours are best in summer and the rocks are as red as blood.'

Wayne couldn't wait another moment. He clenched his right fist and punched. Punched the window in which the ranges were mirrored. Punched and punched. His blood spurted out over the shattered glass. Tourists screamed.

Publican, police, first aid, a rushed ride to hospital. Wayne knew little of it. He only knew the pain. The pain of his people who had lost their land, their heritage, their hope.

Wayne spent the next two months in hospital. An alien world of disinfected orderliness and minuted routine, uniformed doctors and nurses, tedious treatment and physiotherapy for the cut tendons in his right hand.

Relief came through the old people he occasionally found tucked under the starched sheets, the Yuras of the ranges. Their fading eyes looked back beyond their lifetime. They could see the ranges as they had been for forty thousand years, strong in spirit and truth. Their ears could hear the stories they had heard their grandparents tell by the camp-fires in the star-filled nights: stories of crow and kingfisher; of snake – male and female; and of eagle. They knew and they believed. And they shared their faith with the young man, groping his way through pain and rejection, loss and despair.

So Wayne was healed in mind and heart, and the doctors who had predicted that he would not be able to use his right hand again were amazed at what he could do.

The scar will always be there. But Wayne is too busy to see it. He works now among the old people in a Yura hostel in the port, where pelicans glide on the shimmering water and eagles can sometimes be seen on the horizon as they soar towards the ranges.

ZELDA
Emily Rodda

Her name was Zelda. That was the first thing about her. Let's face it, it's not the most ordinary name in the world, is it? I know lots of kids have unusual names. But it doesn't seem to matter with them. I mean, you wouldn't say Blaise, or Makela, or Sion were ordinary names. It was just that Zelda didn't ... just didn't suit her name. Or maybe she did. She was as odd as it was. Maybe that was the trouble. Blaise and Sion and Makela – they were just like everyone else. But Zelda was different.

If I said that to Mum she'd say, 'What do you mean, "different"?' And I'd say something like, 'Well, she has this long hair that she wears in a bun. Black hair. In a bun. With a hairnet over it. And she's got a very fat face, and white skin that looks sort of thick. And her nails are really long and cut into these points, you know, like Auntie Meg's.'

And Mum'd say, in that irritating, reasonable way she has, 'People don't all have to look alike, you know, Jess. You never used to be so conservative.'

'It's not just what she looks like, Mum,' I'd say. 'It's what she's like. It's ...' And then I'd give up, because I couldn't really say what it was that made Zelda odd kid out. But that's what she was. From our first day in Year Seven, that's what she was.

We were all from different schools. All girls. Some people had friends who'd come up from primary with them. Most didn't. But after the first few days most of us had found someone to have lunch with, or talk to in class, or whatever. But that was when I noticed Zelda. She was always by herself. She'd get to school alone, go from class to class by herself, sit alone, reading or just staring into space, at lunchtime. And, you know, it wasn't as if she was actually shy, I don't think. Or not in the usual way, anyway. Shy kids take longer than the others to, you know, get warmed up, and link up with a group, but you can tell they feel shy and want to, and you know that eventually they'll get talking with someone or other and that'll get them started. Harriet, one of my friends, was like that.

But with Zelda you didn't get that feeling. You didn't get any feeling about her at all, really. It was like she was a little drop of oil paint and all the rest of us were drops of water, in a glass. She was just separate, and different, and you just wouldn't know what she was feeling or thinking about.

Somehow you couldn't imagine Zelda having parents, or a house, or anything like that. Well, you could imagine her having them, I suppose, but you couldn't imagine what her parents would be like, or how she'd talk to them. I could imagine her sitting in her bedroom, though. Sitting at a desk in front of a window, I used to think, with her homework in front of her. She'd be looking out the window, her big, white face quite still, like it used to look mostly in class, or in the playground, and you wouldn't know what she was thinking about.

Well, anyway, after a few weeks had gone by and everyone was getting really settled down and confident, the class had sort of divided naturally into groups. You know how it happens. And one of these groups had a couple of kids in it I really didn't like. Their names were Berwyn and Michelle. To be honest, it wasn't quite that I didn't like them, I suppose. It was that I was scared of them. I suppose that sounds stupid.

I don't mean they were scary like they'd hit you on the head with a brick and run off with your lunch money, or that sort of thing. They were scary to me because they were really, sort of, glamorous – you know? They were really good looking, for a start, and they looked older and trendier than anyone else. And they knew things. They knew how things were done. I mean, on day one at high school we all turned up with shiny black clodhopper shoes, and skirts down to our knees and white school shirts from Grace Brothers, and everything. And somehow or other they'd known in advance they'd get away with black canvas shoes and big white T-shirts from the markets, and school skirts hitched half-way up their thighs, and they'd come along looking really smooth. I mean, even if I'd known about how to make the uniform look trendy, Mum wouldn't have let me do it. Not on the first day. Not in a fit.

And Berwyn and Michelle, Berwyn especially, never did anything stupid, or embarrassing. They were never, like, too serious about anything, either. If you're too serious about things, or try too hard at things, it leaves you, sort of, open, you know? You can end up looking like an idiot. People can laugh at you, and send you up. Berwyn and Michelle knew that. I think they must have known it since kindergarten, they were so good at being cool.

The thing was, they despised anyone who wasn't like them. And that was what scared me. I would've liked to be like them, but I knew I wasn't, and I couldn't make myself not care about what they thought of me. I was scared of their superior little smiles, and the way they didn't feel they had to be friendly, or even polite, to other people, and the sarcastic things they said when someone irritated them and the way they whispered to one another, laughing behind their hands, and looking at you.

That was Berwyn and Michelle. The rest of the group weren't quite so cool. There were some gigglers among them, and others of them you could talk to okay, when they were by themselves. When they were by themselves they were quite nice, really. But when they were with Berwyn and Michelle they whispered behind their hands and tittered and said smart, cool things to each other, and flicked their hair back, and stared at you as if you were weird, or your nose was snotty or something.

Well, this day I'm talking about we had a double English period before lunch. Our English teacher that year was Mrs Stephenson, who was also our class teacher. She was nice, and didn't yell or anything, and she was very keen on creative writing. I liked that, so I looked forward to English, usually. Since the beginning of term she'd been getting us to write descriptions of a place, a person, an animal, and so on. This day she said she wanted us to spend the second period writing a description of ourselves – not in the first person, but as though someone else was writing it. She said it was a rather difficult exercise, but she wanted us to try it.

Some kids groaned, and I saw Berwyn and Michelle look at each other and raise their eyebrows in that bored way they had, but no one mucked up on Mrs Stephenson, so eventually we all settled down and started writing. She was right. It's much harder than you'd think, writing about yourself – what you look like and everything. It makes you feel embarrassed. I mean, I think I look quite good, but I didn't want Mrs Stephenson to think I was conceited or anything. And then I couldn't really remember what I did look like, somehow – which sounds ridiculous, but I mean, you just try it! It's really hard, no matter how many times you've looked in a mirror. Anyway, somehow I filled up a page, and I guess it was okay. But I could hardly stand to read over what I'd written. It was really, sort of, personal and embarrassing.

Mrs Stephenson usually collected any writing we'd done at the end of the period, but this time she said she'd like us to read over what we'd written for homework, and make any changes we thought might improve it. She said she'd collect our papers after roll-call the next day. I stuffed my essay into my folder and went out with everyone else for lunch. It was Geography with Mrs Fox in the same room after.

At lunch everyone was talking about the exercise. Some people said it was boring. Other people, like me, said it was really hard. Berwyn and Michelle and that group said it was pointless, and typical of Mrs Stephenson, who was a complete dag and wore hopeless clothes – and they started making up a description of her, all about her varicose veins and support stockings and permed hair. I don't know what Zelda thought about the essay, because as usual she was sitting by herself right away from the crowd, eating her sandwiches. She wasn't reading that day, just staring into space, chewing, chewing, chewing.

I saw Berwyn look at Zelda and nudge Michelle. She whispered something and Michelle grinned. They walked over to the rubbish bin near where Zelda was sitting and tossed in their papers. Then Michelle started to make these moo-ing noises. Berwyn was killing herself laughing and all the other kids in their group, plus quite a few of the others, started giggling too. But Zelda didn't turn her head. Maybe she didn't hear. Maybe she didn't know the noises were aimed at her. Maybe she did, and didn't care. You couldn't tell with Zelda.

Berwyn and Michelle walked back to their gang and got a hero's welcome. They all went off in a huddle, and every now and then for the rest of lunchtime you'd hear a loud moo, and a chorus of giggles, from their spot under the pepper tree. I thought it was pretty pathetic, actually, and so did some of my friends. Mean, too, even though Zelda didn't seem to know what was going on, or care.

It was quite a hot day, that day, and I remember feeling really slow and heavy when Harriet and I walked back into the classroom after lunch. It had been so bright outside that everything looked dim, although the lights were on. We hadn't hurried, and there were already quite a few kids in the room. I remember really clearly seeing Berwyn and Michelle and some of the others standing in a little group round one of the desks. Berwyn was reading something aloud, and the others were collapsing with laughter. One of them, Sylvia, turned and looked round as Harriet and I came in. Her face was bright pink, and tears were actually streaming down her face, she was laughing so much.

They were at Zelda's desk, reading her description of herself. Berwyn had the paper in her hand.

Suddenly I felt myself blushing red, blushing really badly, so my cheeks burned. My whole stomach seemed to turn over, and I felt sick.

I can't explain to you how awful the feeling was. Or why it was so awful. Or why, when I realised Zelda wasn't in the room, hadn't come in yet, I acted the way I did. I mean, I didn't even know Zelda, or like her, or anything. But suddenly it seemed to me as though I was watching someone absolutely helpless being, sort of, invaded by something not human. Suddenly it was like Zelda wasn't the odd kid out at all, but part of me, and Harriet, and all the other people in the world who weren't cool, and cruel, and fearless.

So I went up to Berwyn, who I'd hardly even spoken to

before, and took the paper out of her hand. I said, 'That's not yours,' and I put the paper behind my back.

She looked surprised, really surprised, and then she smiled really sarcastically and shook her head and said, 'Jessica, you're red as a beetroot.'

But Michelle said, 'Who do you think you are, Jessie Simons. Give that back!' And she made a grab for the paper.

I wouldn't give it up, though, and I pushed past them and shoved the essay back in Zelda's folder and stood there, sweating and blushing, with my heart beating furiously, and after a while they all melted back to their own places, because they could hear Mrs Fox and the rest of the class coming down the corridor.

So I went back to my desk too, and sat down. My knees were trembling and I could feel my shirt soaking wet on my back and under my arms. I didn't look at anyone, not at Harriet or anyone. Zelda came in with the others and sat down, and though a few people giggled no one said or did anything – to me or to her.

Zelda sat at her desk, and looked at Mrs Fox, waiting for her to start the lesson. She didn't know what had happened. She didn't have any idea that she'd been invaded. She was as separate from me and the rest of us as ever, with her small blank eyes, and her pointy fingernails. She didn't know that for a moment we'd been sisters, and faced an enemy together.

The next morning Mrs Stephenson collected our descriptions, and a few days later we got them back. I got an A for mine, and she put 'Some nice touches, Jessica,' on the bottom. I sometimes wonder what Zelda got. I saw a few sentences of it, when I put it back in the folder. Zelda had written, with very curly loops, in fine black pen: 'She has lustrous black hair that falls in a rich cascade to her waist. Her hair is hardly ever cut, only to take off split ends. She wears shoes with heels about four centimetres high ...'

Zelda left our school the next year, and I don't know where she went after that. For some reason I often think about her, and wonder what happened to her. Berwyn and Michelle and the others haven't ever forgotten what I did that day, I don't think. Well, I guess they have in one way – they wouldn't, probably, give someone like me a second thought, once the first excitement was over. But I suppose what I mean is that where some of the kids I go round with are invited to their parties, and things like that, I never am. I think that day they wrote me off forever as uncool, and a goody-goody, and maybe a bit mad, and that was that, even though now they've forgotten the thing that started it all.

I have my own friends, though, and I don't care about Berwyn and Michelle. And I'm not scared of them anymore, either. I haven't been, since that day.

It seems to me that growing up is a bit like waking up, bit by bit. You go along, dreaming, thinking you're awake and that you understand how things are, and you're seeing things clearly. And then something happens, or you read something, or someone says something to you, and you blink, and suddenly the world's more in focus than it was before, and you realise you haven't been properly awake at all.

Probably that's why I remember Zelda, and that day. That day was one of my 'waking up' times. I understood a few more things after that.

Not that I understood about Zelda. She was as much a mystery to me after that day as she ever was – well, more, in fact. But somehow I got a bit more of the picture about the world, and how I fitted into it. What side I was on, in fact.

Do you know what I mean?

NOT FOR THE EAR OF ALICE
Ivan Southall

Rebecca fearing that she'd reverted to infancy. Or to some other equally revolting condition. Grumbling to herself that none of this would be fit for the ear of Alice.

Coming along behind the two of them like an obedient child. Rebecca Stirling! The wild one! Laden with sleeping bags and water bags and sundry bits. A night in the sticks with the snakes and the spooks fast approaching.

Engrossing expectation. Nothing but a flutter of nylon between her bare head and the perils of the universe.

In the company of this immature couple bent upon some folly of their middle age. And not long past she'd been clapping her flippers in appreciation! With tears in her eyes and a heart as big as a barrel bulging with sentiment. Thus voluntarily pledging obedience to the whims of crackpot parents and to the greater but unseen host of ancestors surviving in her veins, these uncounted unknowns, these largely un-washed and disreputable people milling around within. Dis-quieting concept. Disgusting.

Not in a hundred years would a word of it be getting to Alice! So the treasure that Rebecca found for herself came despite herself, and by surprise.

Dad (hardly forty minutes past) slowing down, pulling off the sealed road onto the gravelled strip at the side.

'This is it. And what d'you know! There the old place stands. Not in the spirit of the pyramids though.'

Crushed quartz there, at the side of the road, as hard as flint, glinting still in the low rays of the sun, already having caught Rebecca's road-weary eye, though first mined a cen-tury gone in what some called the demented hunt for gold. Now, the spoils, the rubble, the left-overs, in this part of the world, willy-nilly, made into roads.

'How much gold, Dad?' (A courtesy question.)

Few were they among the living who'd know. Fewer still among the dead. That's what Dad said. It was very much that kind of day.

He was stopping the Ford, his shoulders sagging from fatigue, relieved that Happy Valley was close now. His face the old tell-tale grey. Was he ever to do anything the easy way? He'd driven 210 kilometres on top of a day's work and wasn't well. Rebecca was always the first to know.

'This couldn't be,' Mum said.

Incredulity in her voice. As if this landscape would never have dared to be the birthplace of any family embracing her, even by marriage.

'Happy Valley?' she said. 'You'd be joking if I didn't know you better.'

A yellow sadness out there. A flatness. Perhaps a country-side differing little through the ages. Perhaps littered always with heaps of waste and fractured stone. And bearing awful wounds still, as if recent plagues had swept through, though the last mine closed in 1903. Traffic instead, in plenty, heading for where people wished more to be.

Things like this Rebecca also knew.

Stage coaches clattering through. Gold escorts. Buckboards. Horseless carriages. Harley Davidsons. Holdens. MGs. Now, in the warm evening, the big Ford, cobalt blue, transmission in park, engine idling.

Poised.

Livestock not visible out there. Fence lines barely a few posts leaning. Not an occupied house this side of the horizon. A touch away, the ruin.

'Freeman's,' Dad said. Not with a sigh to be heard. Only to be felt. Rebecca feeling it, for some reason, and understanding.

'Looking just like last time,' Dad said. 'Thirteen children born to the Freemans.' (Oh yes, Rebecca knew.) 'Three only to survive. You've heard of Joan. The singer who never made it and deserved better. You've heard of Bruce and his exploit in the Boer War. The medal going to his NCO. You've heard of young Jock, battling for an honest crust, cutting wood in the bush.'

Dad pausing: Rebecca waiting on the outburst.

'Jock murdered for his pitiful small change. I spare you the absurdity of how much.'

It was time he filed the tale and threw away the key. Time he grew out of it. Always upsetting himself, Rebecca wondering why, for it happened back in the dark ages when he wasn't even alive.

The ruin out there: exhausted grey timbers peeling away, chimneys off the vertical, roofing iron rusted out; the lot, by some mystery or magic, held a moment short of collapse, though abandoned even by tramps in 1932.

Something else that Rebecca knew.

The first such saddened house she'd ever seen. The

115

thought that it was deeply saddened coming upon her unawares. If it had fallen years ago, how much less awful now it would have been.

'The turn-off?'

Dad actually questioning the credentials of the landscape he'd presented to his captive pair.

'Where's my turn-off?'

'The famous turn-off?' Mum said. 'You wouldn't be looking for it here?'

'Of course I am. Goes down through the Freeman's, as you know. Great lumps and chunks of quartz. Put down in the 1850s with right-of-way for all time. Put down like a Roman road.'

'Yes,' Mum said, 'but a little less permanent, I'd say, wouldn't you? No turn-off now.'

'There's got to be!'

'Fine time, Roy, to discover your destination has moved. You should've checked before we left home.'

'Checked where? It's been twenty years. Last time I was here we hadn't met, you and me. Checked with whom?'

Rebecca didn't care for the trend. Mum and Dad hassling each other again. A close-up, then, of his face in the rear vision mirror. Taking off his sunglasses. Squeezing his eyes shut as if pains were in his head.

'On a stack of Bibles,' he said, 'I swear I'm exactly where I'm supposed to be! But you wouldn't be thanking me if we set out on foot to go down from here. What's happened to the turn-off?'

'There's the symbolic tent to erect,' Mum said. 'I remind you of it. And the camp-fire meal to cook. The idea of sitting out the night in the car debating the fate of the turn-off and listening to the rumble of empty stomachs doesn't grip me.'

'Doesn't grip me either,' Dad said.

'You wouldn't be feeling ill again?'

'I'll take you somewhere, Julie. I don't intend to sit here debating the fate of the turn-off or the state of my health indefinitely. No. I'm not feeling ill again.'

But he was.

Rebecca knew.

'I need a break,' he said, 'that's all, to collect my limited wits. Does anyone mind? I appear to be under attack. This was to have been an important moment for me. Very long awaited.'

Important for some, Rebecca agreed.

'It's shaping up, Julie, to be a non-event. Give thought to a wait of twenty years going down the tube. A pain of conscience of twenty years standing. Nagging at me every day.'

I can hear my Mum, Rebecca thought, singing her little song. *And so say all of us!*

But she was instantly sorry, for there were her dad's clouded eyes in the mirror conveying a degree of distress he might not have meant to show her at any time.

He wasn't a bad guy. And he was in trouble. For his tediously sacred spot must have been tantalisingly near, but inexplicably far away.

Was it possible he'd come too far? Or gone not far enough? How much really might he forget in twenty years? Rebecca well knew how much he could forget in a week.

'The Stirlings,' he liked to say, 'originated in that little tent at Happy Valley with the birth of my grandmother. Give it your consideration. My great-grandmother attended only by my great-grandfather. She at eighteen and he not twenty. And he in the father of all panics. What a panic it must've been.'

A panic that lives on in the family to this day, was Rebecca's unspoken view.

'Sooner or later,' Dad had been saying to her since birthday two or three, 'I'll be taking you there.'

One of the more distant mileposts of childhood. Not reached in childhood. ('Don't call me *child*! I'm fourteen!') A milepost perhaps not reached now either.

'The family,' (Dad's words), 'as we know it, wasn't recognisable until my grandmother came into being. Eldest of seven. And what are you, my girl? Eldest of one. Not that anyone round here's to blame for that. The Almighty, in His wisdom, ordains. I'll put you on the spot where my great-grandfather pitched his tent. The very spot, give or take a dozen steps.'

It was the speech for delivering on wedding anniversaries, as well as on birthdays before they blew out the candles.

'Pitched his tent and built his house of hardwood felled on his own acres and split with his own axe. I'd ask you to think it through. And built of bricks baked in the kiln he constructed for himself. An achievement for a lad of nineteen. More than I could ever do. Nothing much left but the stumps and the bricks after the big fires went through; '39 or '62. Half a chimney. Bricks breaking down to powder. Lumps of fused glass. The well he dug. Dry.

'You'd reckon no one had been there in a thousand years.

'I, too, was nineteen. Waited for centuries to turn nineteen. But the symbolism that charmed me was the symbolism that overwhelmed me. I couldn't bear it above a minute or two. Thinking of what I was and of what they'd been. I have a memory of running from it. Running like a rabbit. Every way at the same time. Later I wondered if ever I'd find my little Mini again. I needed to. I owed a thousand on it when a thousand was a fortune.'

The driving side door of the big Ford swung open, Dad sliding out. Still looking grey. And tense. And went striding ahead about thirty or forty paces. Back he came.

'They've widened the road!'

Clipping each word. Accenting it with anger.

'They've cut off the track to the Valley. As if it never mattered. As if the Valley had never been there. Can't you hear them? *What the hell's this bit of rubble?*'

A change in Mum. A visible change in her manner. 'Oh, Roy, I *am* sorry.'

'Can't you see them? Putting the dozer through it!'

'I suppose I can. But I'd like to see you much less excited about it.'

'They've cut it off from us. It'll be over there. Over the ditch. God knows how far over. What's wrong with these two-bit engineers? What gives them licence to ride rough-shod over the things that've made the country?'

'I know, Roy. I know. And I sympathise, I do. But calm yourself. Please. I'd hoped for something of this expedition. But I hadn't hoped to be widowed here. In my thirties.'

Rebecca heard herself crying out, 'Don't get so hot and bothered, Dad. You know you mustn't. It can never be worth it, Dad.'

Dad leaning against the car. Glancing from his anguished wife to his anguished daughter. Everyone wondering where this emotional turn of events had come from. Dad looking embarrassed about it and trying not to show that he was labouring for breath.

'It's worth it,' he said, as quietly and as evenly as he was able. 'It's the reason we've come after all these years of vacillation. I needed to do it. I still need to do it. I believe I've always known more about my health than the doctor. But I've been scared. I need you both to help me bridge the ditch.'

He indicated the paddocks.

'I want the fenceposts. I want everything we can move from there. I want it all in the ditch. We build up a crossing. Then we go over and take our road down into Happy Valley.'

'Can it be as important as that?' Mum said.

'Of all people, do you really have to ask?'

Rebecca went on asking, just the same, over and over.

Asking inside: Does it matter? Can't you hear what Mum's saying to you? Does it matter like life and death? Like feeding the hungry? Like healing the sick? Does it really, really matter? Wouldn't it be better letting her drive and turn the car about and go back home before something terrible happens?

Mum getting out, as if to change seats and do as Rebecca hoped. But standing, a hand at one hip, kicking at the crushed quartz under one shoe. 'I don't approve of making crossings of fenceposts. Or crossings of anything else. We're looking at a level of stress that'd send your doctor out through the roof. With no guarantee we'd get the car safely across or safely anywhere else. But if you want to do it on foot, I'll accompany you.'

Rebecca aghast.

On foot?

Does she know how far? Does he know? This old wreck of a house might have nothing to do with the Freemans. Maybe the Goldsteins lived here. How can he remember back twenty years? It's pre-history. He can't remember what he did last Sunday.

'What of the car?' Dad said.

A superb point, in Rebecca's opinion. A masterstroke for sanity. Three hearty cheers for good old Henry Ford. Then Mum was saying, 'Well, honey, what of the car?'

Even Dad a bit taken aback. 'Are you suggesting we leave it here? Until later? Until tomorrow or the day after? It could be stolen. It could be stripped.'

'So it gets stolen. So it gets stripped. Or it isn't touched. What's ultimately important?'

Rebecca having a private fit.

Dad's shoulders rising and falling as if he were about to break down and weep, and Rebecca, unexpectedly, experiencing the electric touch of his hand though it was reaching out to Mum. Just as suddenly, she was giving way to the shivers, having to blink back tears, having to listen to the outraged remnant of her other self: 'They're out of their little minds. We're all raging mad. Not a hint of this ever, oh never never, for the ear of Alice.'

Rebecca grumbling to herself. Laden like a pack-pony. Sweating like one. Sleeping bags, water bags, and sundry bits.

I ought to flick my tail. I ought to whinny. What I feel like I might as well be.

'Can't be far now,' Dad was saying, 'I've got the shakes inside. All of a tremble. Like an early warning signal.' More like a one-man talks programme! He was talking the bark off the trees. 'Look out for plums. Cherry plums. Gone wild. Thickets of them. When you see them, we'll be there.'

Rebecca tripping and stumbling across the abandoned lumps and chunks of quartz. The pot-holes and ridges and tussocks and ruts. Even the scrub, becoming more and more invasive. Even the little stunted trees springing out of rock like weeds.

The bare, sad paddocks back there somewhere. Freeman's back there, too, hardly a memory except that it had been less difficult across the flats near the car. Cryptic note taped to the inside of the windscreen. *Vehicle unsafe. Back soon.* 'Psychology,' Dad explained, 'and practicality.' You'd hardly know the man. Committing a vital part of the distributor to his deepest pocket.

Shadows lengthening. Daylight worn almost into the ground. Narrow gullies backing up on either side. As wild as if they'd never known the hand of man. After rain they'd be running high. They'd be roaring. But not now. Heaps of mullock in the bush, yellow and grey. All those dark forgotten holes below. All those dreams underground. Brooding?

'Best foot forward, Rebecca. Can't be far.'

It wouldn't need to be.

121

Dad chattering on ahead. Laden like a pack-horse. Excited in a way she'd never seen. Not grey about the face. Not flushed. Not breathing in any obvious, worrying way. Not ill.

Which was food for thought. For very serious thought.

Dad still chattering: 'What use would the car have been? We'd have wrecked it. We would've, you know. Things look different; much rougher down here than last time.'

Rebecca grumbling along with her other self: not too different, I hope. I couldn't *bear* it if there were two roads and we'd picked the wrong one. We're skating awful close to the dark. Things are getting spooky all round.

Mum, laden like a pack-camel, looking back. Gesturing to Rebecca with an encouraging hand. With every appearance of radiance. She'd be lighting up the place instead of day. Fancy ever wondering how Dad came to fall for her back when the world was young. Taking after her, like the carbon copy, mightn't be the big calamity after all.

Dad stopping. Half-raising a hand. Standing there, as if about to prophesy. Choosing not to.

Rebecca having a kind of heart failure.

The thickets. The plums. The cherry plums. Shouldn't she just have known! There they were, among the spookiest of the spooky bits. A chimney, most of it down. Copses of second growth timber. Gigantic mounds of briar roses. White lilies, like a painting, disturbingly large.

Dad's hand eerily, in silence, passing through a wide arc; coming to rest against Mum.

Rebecca trying to call: 'I vote we go home. I don't like it here.' But the words wouldn't come.

Rebecca attempting to add: 'Let's chuck it, Dad. It's crazy. Now I know why you ran.' But nothing was said.

Rebecca beginning to feel too heavily burdened. Beginning to feel too young. Sleeping bags too heavy. Water bags leaden. All the sundry bits, heavy, heavy.

Even the breezes laden with pollen.

And the sounds upon the evening. Heavy wings beating. Big birds calling in low registers. Like organ notes at funerals.

Wearily, so wearily, Rebecca sitting at the edge of her heap of sleeping bags. Sitting on her milepost at childhood's end. Having a good weep.

Watching Dad. Watching Mum. Watching them shed their loads as she had done.

Hand in hand, Mum and Dad, walking slowly in, Rebecca's treasure.

Oh, Alice.

SLEEPWALKMAN
Ted Greenwood

*. . . And it is essential that all of you at this school, and I mean
ALL, everyone, yes, even you, Barrott, there in the third row
not listening but preferring to amuse yourself with something
under the seat . . . even for you, Barrott, it is essential that
you understand the effect that behaviour such as that reported to have taken place at the station has on the image of the
school.*

*Not too many years ago, the reputation of this school was
unflattering to say the least. For the last few years, we have
worked hard to have that sad state of affairs repaired, and
I do not want incidents like last Friday's to signal a return
to the bad old days. Standards are not imposed on you
merely because the staff want to lean on you, but to ensure*

*responsible behaviour, behaviour the community is entitled
to expect from its local school . . .*

*I hope, Kosta, that your whispering indicates your under-
standing of what I am saying, and that you have nudged your
mate Selley there to likewise pay attention to what I am
trying to get through to you . . .*

Boy, does old Savo go on! When he gets wound up like he
is now, I just switch off. He sends you off. It could be all that
walking he does. There he goes again. Five paces to that side,
then turn. Now . . . one, two, three, four, five back again. Now
he'll stop. Yes. Now turn. Yes. And then off he goes again.
Hypnotists are supposed to do something like that – have
something on the end of a chain and swing it from side to
side and make you keep staring at it until you go into a
trance.

*. . . I am not going to ask those responsible for this incident
to identify themselves, but I want them to know that their
behaviour has put the clock back several years to when . . .*

That's it. A clock. Savo's like a pendulum of one of those
grandfather clocks, except that he takes ages to swing from
side to side. Maybe it's what he's going on about. Half the
school couldn't care less about whatever it is. He puts in
those long words just to make it sound big deal.

*. . . and yes, Hurst, we treat this kind of incident with the
utmost seriousness. It is not a subject for the amusement of
you and that little clique of jokers you seem to always gather
around you.*

It's his voice. It doesn't go up and down. He just drones on
and on and on. I don't think he's looking at me, not with that
big log Bicks in front. Savo won't pick on me. Or will he? He
might see me when he turns to go back the other way. He
won't notice me if I stay still. That's how he picked out
Hursty and those others. They moved. If you don't move, he
doesn't notice you. I wonder how long he's going to keep
raving on? Still, why should I care? He's taking up Maths

126

time. Look at Kitey. She's bored, I bet. All the staff look bored. Can't blame them. Wicker's actually grinning. We wouldn't be allowed to get away with that. I wonder does Savo give the staff the treatment we get from him? There should be some invention you can just switch on that switches you off without making you look as if you've fallen asleep. Your eyes would stay open, you'd look wide awake, but you'd be tuned-out. Then you wouldn't have to put up with listening to the stuff he's giving us right now.

. . . The tone of this school is something we all contribute to in our separate ways . . .

Tone. His tone would send anyone off to sleep. With my invention, you'd still be watching him pace up and down, but you wouldn't have to listen to him. It'd be a bit like seeing him on the telly with the sound turned down. My gadget would have an in-built memory, so that if he suddenly jumped on you to answer one of his stupid questions, you'd hear a bleep and then you'd be awake again, and not only that, you'd know what the question had been and, better still, you'd be given a decent answer to trot out.

. . . Each of our actions, whether good or bad, influences the reputation not only of the individual concerned, but of the whole school body. Therefore . . .

The body. Yes, my tune-out would have to be worn somewhere on the body. It could be like Uncle Les's hearing aid. The ear would be a good place to put it. The closer to the brain the better. You couldn't stick it up your nose, and you'd look a bit weird with some gadget strapped on to your skull all the time. No, it would have to be made to stick in one ear. No wires though. You could have some kind of control hidden in your pocket, but no daggy-looking wires going from it up to your ear.

. . . and in our endeavours to maintain a reasonable standard of discipline, I am sure that we have the support of your parents . . .

Who else besides school-kids would want to buy one of the gadgets? I might be able to sell one to Dad. He's always moaning about how boring it is going into the city and back every day by train. He could use one to tune-out soon after he got on the train, and he could stay tuned-out to the end of the trip and then tune-in again. But wait a minute, what if he didn't press the control to wake up again? He'd stay on the train just sitting there like a zombie, staring into space. They'd have to get the police or doctors to try and wake him up again. They might think he was on drugs or something. Gee, Dad would love that – suspected of being on drugs. Poor guy. I'd have to make sure there was some kind of timer and alarm to wake him up. He'd have to set it to go off just before the train was due to reach the city. That'd work . . . unless there was some kind of hold-up on the line. Dad says that there's often some strike or break-down to make the trains late. Oh well, then he'd just wake up a bit early, that's all, and that wouldn't matter. Better than staying asleep and going past your stop and being arrested or something.

. . . At this stage I don't believe it is necessary to call a special meeting, or to do anything more than include a report of this incident in the monthly newsletter to parents . . .

I'm not sure when Mum could use one of the tune-outs . . . She doesn't like driving to work, but she couldn't tune-out while she's driving. Maybe when cars are automatically driven and you just sit in them and programme them to take you where you want to go, maybe then she could use one, because driving then could be even more boring than going by train every day. You'd see all these people choofing along reading their newspapers and the cars all obeying traffic signals and turning without the drivers doing anything.

Right now, Mum could only use a tune-out at those meetings she says she has to go to at her work. She might sell them to all the others who have to go to the meetings. They'd all sit there staring straight ahead. But who'd do the talking? At meetings someone has to do the talking. They'd have to take it in turns to be awake and have their say, and then they could tune-out to all the boring stuff the others said. They wouldn't fight and argue like Mum says they nearly always seem to do.

. . . *How the wider community regards this school is of great importance to me and to all the staff . . .*

Who else would buy one? Not Uncle Les, that's for sure. He's tuned-out most of the time anyway. I bet he doesn't mind being a bit deaf with Auntie Ruth around all the time. I'd give her a free tune-out if I lived at their place, just to shut her up. I suppose it's because Uncle Les is a bit deaf that she talks a lot when we go to visit them. Boy, can she talk. Even louder than Savo. But it wouldn't be fair to shut her up. She'd be lost . . . Oh, I know who might buy one. I reckon I could sell one to rubber-lips Sneeks over there. She'd be able to record everything we whisper about without leaving her desk. She'd love that. No more creeping around the library spying on kids through the shelves. No more hiding to catch someone tossing things across the carrels. She'd have a record of everything that went on in the library.

I'm not sure she'd want to be tuned-out though. She looks spaced out already sometimes when you go up to change a book. You can't tell what she's thinking behind those thick glasses. But what an easy life it'd be for her. But if she was tuned-out, how would she manage when someone came to borrow a book? You'd go up to the desk and all you'd get would be the big freeze. I suppose she could pile all that kind of work on to that other funny little one that helps her some-times. Sneeks mightn't want to trust her with that. She's always butting in to show the little one how to use the keyboard at the desk. I've seen her. But anyway, she wouldn't have to be tuned-out for the whole time. That's the good thing about my invention. You could use it just whenever you felt like escaping.

I've heard Sneeks say that the library would be a great place without students in it, so she could tune-out when the place was full of us. She doesn't look as if she likes us being there. I think she'd rather nothing went off the shelves at all. She'd like to keep all the books and tapes locked away. Then she wouldn't have to have anything to do with us. She got mad that time when I was looking for stuff on Galileo and I pulled those two big books out, and then put them back again. As if I couldn't see where they'd just come from. What a pain she is! Teachers are always going on about making use of the library, and they go and put someone like Sneeks Callaghan in charge ... No, I wouldn't sell a tune-out to Sneeks. Instead, I'd sell one to the little one. Yes, that's it. I'd sell one to her, and then Sneeks would have to do everything. Little One could go into that glassed-off part and just sit and stare out into the library. She'd have an easy time, and get paid for it.

. . . The state of the yard is, once again, pretty untidy. Littering is not something that . . .

Well there's one thing for sure, I wouldn't have to sell one to old Andy. He's got it easy already. The other cleaner, that fat guy, must do nearly the whole school by himself. You never see him sitting in that little room of theirs down by the gym, but every time I've been past, Andy's been in there, puffing. Maybe that's the only place he's allowed to smoke. You can hardly see him through the fug. Sometimes, he doesn't even seem to notice you're there when you say 'Hi' to him. What a big bludge. Tuned-out all day, every day.

. . . Now, on to a less serious matter – Open Day. I would hope that everyone will make it their business to advertise . . .

I might be on the news: 'A major breakthrough in relaxation technology has been achieved with the announcement today of the launching of the TUNE-OUT. This amazing device can be worn by anyone, and at the press of a button, it will send them into a relaxing sleep . . .'

Or I could be on the telly: 'In the studio today we have Michael Le Fevre, the young inventor of TUNE-OUT, and Professor Ted Savoury, electronics expert, to comment on the significance of this invention to society. First, Michael. Michael, are you wearing your hypnotic device right here in the studio?'

'Yes. But of course I haven't got it switched on.'

Big laugh from the audience.

'Before we came on camera, you told me that you had placed it in your ear. I must say it is very well camouflaged. Would you take it out and show our audience the relative size of this truly amazing instrument? ... There you are, viewers, there it is in the palm of his hand – hardly visible, especially as it seems to be covered with something that looks like the colour and texture of skin. Amazing! And yet, in that small package, there are thousands of tiny complex circuits which, when activated, send the wearer off into a deep, hypnotic sleep. Just incredible! Yet more incredible still, while the wearer remains in a trance, the instrument records everything going on close by, and transfers that automatically to the mind of the wearer. Unbelievable! ... Perhaps we could ask the professor here to explore some of the possibilities and applications of this invention, by putting to our young inventor questions scientists might want answered before giving the instrument their seal of approval. Professor?'

'Yes, thank you. Well, young man, you claim that your invention acts like sleeping-pills, but without causing the users to miss out on anything that happens while they are asleep. Is that so?'

'Yes sir, that's what it does.'

'And what brings them out of their relaxed trance?'

'The control button here on this panel you carry in your pocket.'

'Ah, but how can they know that they must press it?'

'I've thought of that. You see here on the control panel that there are twelve different periods of time you can choose to be tuned-out, anything from ten seconds to an hour. Choose your time and the bleeper will automatically go off and wake you up again. If you want longer than an hour, you press this repeat button, and off you go into another trance.'

'May I try it?'

'Sure, Professor.'

'Well, viewers, right before you, the professor has taken the unit from our young inventor, inserted the capsule into his ear, and taken the control panel in his left hand. He has chosen ... is that wise, Professor? He has chosen the full one-hour period to tune-out .... Professor! Professor!! Oh dear, he seems to have gone off immediately. As you see, he's just staring straight ahead ... Just a moment ... he's starting to speak. He's ... would you believe, he sounds as if he's a newsreader. Can't we press the bleeper and wake him up?'

'No, not once he's chosen a time.'

'Oh no, not an hour of him being a newsreader, not a whole hour of it!'

... and your money has to be in by next Thursday, or you won't be going on the trip ...

I still think I could make a fortune with my tune-out, as long as things don't start getting mixed up and people go acting like newsreaders or whatever. Perhaps you can't stop people having nightmares instead of dreams, or just doing nothing in their sleep. The tune-out won't be very popular if people tune-out and then start raving or shouting out. I wouldn't make a fortune out of it then.

What I need is a better name for it, one that'll make every-one feel good when they use it ... the HYPNOSISTER. No. People might think you use it to hypnotise your sister ... DOZEMASTER? No. It's peaceful enough, but it could be the name of a mattress. It's got to sound more electronic than that ... I know. It'd be a bit like carrying round a Walkman, so what about SLEEPWALKMAN? ... 'Buy one today, and look forward to a life free from boring speeches, talks, even an instant cure for headaches and fatigue. Throw away your headache pills and move into the twenty-first century cure: the SLEEPWALKMAN. For relaxed living.'

Le Fevre!

SLEEPWALKMAN ... but people might think it actually gets you sleepwalking.

Le Fevre!!

Le Fevre's SLEEPWALKMAN. It sounds pretty classy ... 'We would like you to accept this award for the most original invention shown in our series *Beyond the twentieth century:* to Michael Le Fevre for his SLEEPWALKMAN.'

Le Fevre!!!

'Yes, sir?'

Just exactly where have you been, boy?

'I'm here, sir.'

I know you are physically here, but are you a part of this school or not? I detect in your bowed head and your slumped posture that you have taken this opportunity to steal a nap. I am sure we would all like to grant ourselves that luxury, but our duties do not allow it. I am compelled to address you on matters of some importance, and I expect you to tune-in on my wavelength, as it were. Do I make myself clear, Le Fevre?

'Yes, sir.'

Then perhaps you can bring yourself to give me the gist of what I have been trying to get across to this assembly, and which you obviously find not worthy of your keenest attention.

'What's 'gist', sir?'

'Gist,' my dear Le Fevre, is the core or the kernel of whatever is being said. Now, can you tell me even a little of what I have been saying?

'Something about what happened at the station.'

Is that all?

'And the Open Day.'

Oh, good. It appears you picked up one or two words here and there. But obviously, there are gaping holes in your memory, Le Fevre. Would it be too much to ask that in future you concentrate for at least eighty per cent of the time, if not for the full hundred?

As I was saying, before I was diverted by our friend Le Fevre's inattention, those students going on the trip to the Centre will . . .

Phew! That was close.

Wherever we are, we are on show, and by the behaviour of these few, so will the rest of the school be judged . . .

Not more of it. Surely Savo can't have anything left to drone on about. But there he goes again . . . one, two, three, four, five, stop. Always five paces. He must count them. Who does he think is listening, anyway?

. . . We always carry responsibility for the good name . . .

It's not a bad name – SLEEPWALKMAN. Still, it might be better if I called it something even more electronic . . .

. . . And I hope you will all remember . . .

What about MEMORYMAN? . . . MEMORYMAX? . . . MEMORYMODEM? . . .

. . . You can't buy a reputation. You have to earn it . . .

I reckon it'd be easy to sell my MEMORYMODEM or SLEEP-WALKMAN or whatever I call it, to just about everyone here, including the staff. Everyone . . .

Apart from old Savo.

RIVER SERPENT
Victor Kelleher

It felt unreal from the start. Not like an ordinary hunting trip. Almost dream-like. For one thing, the day was too perfect: with no wind, the sky clear the air warm without being hot. Also, there was no one about, the surrounding bush oddly deserted. That was until he saw the figure on the raised bank beside the track, perched up there so straight and still that she was more like a rock or tree than a person. He spotted her just as he was about to begin the descent into the gorge – an Aboriginal woman sitting between him and the sun, so all he could see at first was her dark silhouette.

'What's the gun for?' she asked, pointing to the rifle he was carrying.

'Just in case,' he answered uneasily.

'In case of what?'

'I might see a roo or something.'

She shook her head. 'I wouldn't do no shootin' down there if I was you. Not in the gorge.'

'Why not?'

'I wouldn't, that's all.'

It was her tone that made him hesitate.

'What's so special about the gorge?' he asked.

She shrugged. 'I reckon it's just about had enough.'

He didn't really understand that, but again her tone made him pause, and he edged forward, trying for a better view of her face. He was expecting someone old; someone with a scrawny neck and features weathered by sun and wind. But he found to his surprise that she was young. Younger than him in fact. An Aboriginal girl he'd seen at school, from one of the lower forms.

'What d'you know about it anyway?' he said, resenting her advice. 'You're only a kid.'

She didn't answer and he strode on; the track carrying him over the lip of the gorge and down. So that within minutes he was alone again, the day as peaceful as before. Almost too peaceful, for although he stayed alert he saw nothing. Not another living creature. It was more like walking through a painting of the bush than an actual place: the yellow grass unruffled by wind; the trees as straight and still as the girl on the rock; the sky too blue to be real. Like a dream version of the gorge he knew.

That was why his first sight of the river came as such a shock. Because it wasn't perfect like the day itself. It was brown and sluggish, with heaps of gravel lining its banks, from where it had been dredged in the gold rush days. Now, years later, there was nothing precious, nothing gold-like about its bare grey shoreline. The whole river, including its banks, seemed completely dead except for one thing: a faint hint of green just below the surface of the water. Weed, perhaps, or algae, which moved slightly in the current; which occasionally glinted with rainbow colours when it caught the light – as though a huge snake, greenish, but with coloured tips to its scales, were lurking down there.

Curious, he left the track and crawled out across a slab of rock. A deep pool lay directly below him, and when he looked into it carefully something seemed to stir in its depths. More than just the uncoiling of weed. Something so unexpectedly alive that he almost turned and ran.

Instead, he closed his eyes and gripped the rifle more tightly, for reassurance. 'Yabbies,' he thought. 'That's what it'll be, yabbies.' Their backs a similar greenish colour; their armoured bodies capable of glinting in the sunlight.

They were still down there when he looked again. The same rainbow flashes as before. And on impulse he leaned out over the edge of the rock and fired.

The crash of the gunshot destroyed the silence, and immediately the pool erupted in a spray of brown and green. He reloaded and fired again, the noise bouncing off the steep sides of the gorge. The pool churned into foam, as if something were thrashing wildly.

Just for an instant he half-believed that he saw a head, an eye, rearing above the surface. The eye, especially, was so beautiful and terrible that he rolled over hastily and stared up at the empty sky. Except that now it was no longer empty. A tiny black speck had appeared high in the blue. Rapidly it grew into a creature with wings, head, talons. A wedge-tailed eagle that was plummeting down. Towards him! Its talons spread vengefully, its cry somehow giving voice to the nameless thrashing in the river.

As a reflex action he raised the rifle and pulled the trigger. It was an impossible shot, meant only to scare the bird off. And yet amazingly the bullet found its mark. What had been a living bird instantly became a lifeless bundle. In a flurry of feathers it slammed into the rock beside him, bounced over the edge, and dropped into the pool – its limp wings spread like giant fans upon the surface.

He could not believe what he had done for a moment. The day had been so peaceful. More like a . . . For the first time he admitted it: a troublesome idea lingering at the back of his mind right from the outset. That none of this was real; that it was just an unpleasant dream he was having.

As in a dream, he turned to where, high above him, he could see the dark figure of the Aboriginal girl etched against the sky. Had she really been a girl from school, he wondered, or was she the old woman he had first imagined? He shook his head, confused. And what was she doing now? Pointing something at him? Waving?

Again he felt he was caught up in a dream. The sort where you are given no choice about what happens next. For all at once he found he was running down the track; clambering over the heaped gravel at the water's edge; floundering, fully-clothed, out into the pool.

Close up, the eagle was like the river itself: its great flight feathers not simply a brownish-black, but tinted with rainbow hues. The outer, upturned tip of a wing was floating tantalisingly just beyond his reach. He stretched out, the water swirling about his waist, and almost touched it. One more step and he would have been able to drag the bird to the shore. But before his fingers could close, a sudden ripple of current snaked across the pool and drew the bird under. The same current, unbelievably strong, began tugging at him; green tendrils of weed coiling about his ankles and knees.

He floundered desperately – his struggle to keep his balance making him forget about the gun which slipped from his hand. As it sank, leaving behind a thin trail of bubbles, so the current lost some of its force. The tight grip on his feet and legs slackened just long enough for him to scramble towards the shore. Within seconds the current was snatching at his heels once again, but by then he was safe.

Or so he believed as he crawled up onto the gravel bank. He was not quite so confident a minute or two later, because when he next looked up, the once clear sky was marred by a line of black cloud that was advancing rapidly. It blotted out the sun even as he watched, plunging the valley into shadow. Already heavy drops were falling all about him, growing into a downpour and then a deluge that turned the gravel bank to gritty mud. So much water coursing down the sides of the gorge that he could no longer say where the river began and the hillside ended. Dirty brown streams of it rising almost to his knees; the same insistent current catching at him yet again.

With a loud cry he splashed through the rising tide, grabbing at overhanging branches, at long tufts of yellow grass, pulling himself further up the hillside. He glanced behind him once, in time to see a flash of lightning. It was followed by another, so vivid that it completely dazzled him; left him with a brilliant image of a glowing snake-body zig-zagging across the sky. The thunder seemed to add a voice to the image: an angry rumbling that shook the hillside. The rain, meanwhile, continued to pour down, growing ever harder.

He could again feel the river tugging at him and he tried to climb higher, but in the deepening gloom he had lost the path and he was confronted by a vertical cliff. Dashing the water from his eyes, he followed the winding line of the river, half-running through the shallows in an attempt to stay ahead of the current.

Once, he thought he had escaped. A willow grew straight out from the bank, and he jumped for it and swung himself up among the branches. For a while he remained crouched there, the river roaring past below. Then he felt the tree sag as its roots lost their hold, and he had to leap clear before it was dragged under.

He, too, nearly went under. As he fought for some kind of foothold, the lightning flashed once more; and he saw, poised above him, as though about to strike, what he took to be a large serpent head. Only afterwards, when his body collided with the rock and he crawled up onto it, did he realise that what he had glimpsed was probably the crooked branch of a tree. He was tempted to glance back, to make sure, but he lacked the nerve.

'Hold on!' he muttered grimly. 'Just hold on and it'll pass.'

He had told himself that before, during other childhood nightmares. And as on those occasions he knew in his heart that despite his fear nothing really bad could happen to him. Eventually he would wake up in his own room, with the lamp shining peacefully on the table beside his bed.

The thought of the light seemed to bring it into being. He blinked, and there it was, right before him. Not his bedside lamp, but a lighted window, covered only with a flimsy scrap of hessian. The window was part of a tiny shack – a slab hut with a roof half of iron, half of bark strip.

He stumbled towards it. In all the noise and confusion there was no point in knocking, and he punched the door open and staggered inside. An old man was sitting on a rickety chair over near the chimney, a stub of lit candle beside him. His head turned on his scrawny neck, and it was clear straight away, from the gleam in his eyes, that he was mad.

'You're a bit late for the gold,' he said, and jerked a claw-like thumb towards the river. 'She's played out. No more'n a ₁ew pennyweight left. An' I should know. I seen it all. The pannin', the dredgin', the lot.'

He went over and crouched beside the old man. 'We have to get out of here,' he said. 'The river's rising. It's dangerous.'

'Not me,' the man answered, his eyes flashing crazily. 'This 'ere's where I made an' lost me pile. This 'ere's where I'll stay.'

'But the river! And that . . . that . . .'

He could not find the word to describe what he had sensed out there, yet still the man seemed to understand him.

'What, you startin' to believe in it too?' he said with a chuckle. 'You musta been talkin' to the ol' lubra up the hill. What she call it? A rainbow snake or somethin'. No, a serpent, that's it.'

'Come on!' he cried, pulling at the man's skinny body – for murky water was seeping through the slab walls, a wash of it lapping at the doorsill; the whole hut shuddering as the river roared and sucked its way past.

The man shook him off. 'I told her but,' he added slyly. 'Last time I seen the ol' lubra, I says, you can't fool me with no fancy names. Rivers is rivers, I says, an' eels is eels. Never mind how big. Never mind about no rainbow stuff. That's for scarin' the kids.'

There was a crash as something slammed into the side of the hut, and a wave of water gushed in through the door, swirling about their feet. At the window, the hessian was torn aside and the stub of candle blinked out.

He felt for the man's arm and was pushed roughly aside.

'Stories for scarin' the kids,' he heard the old voice repeat as he groped his way to the door and out into the night.

This time the river almost had him: a surge of cold water, oddly slimy to the touch, catching him off balance and forcing him to his knees. Momentarily he went under . . . and felt it! The living presence he had only glimpsed earlier! Powerful coils closing about him; rainbow colours flashing across his darkened vision as he fought for breath.

It was only the knowledge that he was asleep which made that moment bearable. Half-drowned, choking and spluttering, he rose from the churning water; blundered past the sagging wall of the hut and up into the teeming darkness of the hillside. Behind him, the river shrieked out its unforgiveness. The wind answered, howling dementedly; sharp-bladed grass and branches, serpent-toothed, striking at his face and arms. Through it all, he struggled on, telling himself at every step how it would soon be over, soon ...

But another vertical bank confronted him, where a whole section of hillside had been washed away, and now he lacked the will to search out another route. Exhausted, he sank down on the wet grass. With his face pressed close to the ground, he could hear it still – the unfolding coils of the river creeping higher; the slither and rustle of its body moving towards him.

He made one last, unsuccessful effort to rise. Then, beaten by the sheer fury of the storm, he crept into the lee of a rock and curled up on a sodden litter of gum leaves. 'Stories for scarin' the kids.' That's how the old man had described it all. Well, he wasn't much more than a kid himself, and he was scared. All he could do now was wait. Not just for the river to reach him, but for that moment when his ordeal would be over. Shivering with cold and fright, he burrowed deeper into the litter, willing himself to wake; to leave all his terror, all his serpent imaginings behind.

And to his relief his body seemed to respond. He could feel himself drifting away from the hillside; growing numb, detached from the cold and the noise. A single thought, jolting through his weariness, half roused him. The *old* lubra, the man had said. Old! Whereas the figure up on the lip of the gorge had been young. Hadn't she? A girl he knew from school. In which case ... But the effort of thinking the idea through was too much for him. It was better just to drift. To abandon himself to the night, knowing that somewhere on the other side of danger and darkness he would emerge into a very different kind of reality. A snug room lit by a softly shaded lamp.

With a sigh he closed his eyes. Gave himself up. Though only to sleep. A dreamless sleep undisturbed by thoughts of a softly lit room. His body still there on the hillside where he had left it, shivering uncontrollably in the cold night air. While paces from where he lay, the river, like a huge and hungry snake, steadily devoured the valley it had once created; its angry voice filling the night as it slithered nearer.

MISS FABERGÉ'S LAST DAZE
Jenny Wagner

The girls in Miss Fabergé's class cried when she left. Even the boys seemed quieter than usual; their clamour as they crowded round to say goodbye was muted and melancholy, and they signed her going-away card with gruff, tough messages to remember them – or else.

Tracey's friend Marianne cried louder than anyone; and Tracey, who was only a little tougher, drew a pink heart in her autograph book and blew her nose as she got Miss Fabergé to sign it.

She knew she was losing the best teacher in the world. Miss Fabergé was young, sweet-faced and elegant, had Italian shoes with matching handbags, and never worried about homework, or why you were late, or whether you talked in class.

Her replacement, Miss Blackstone, arrived three days later on a wet Monday morning.

Tracey and Marianne, watching from the library window, saw a light-brown station-wagon with rust stains round the doors drive in through the gate marked BUSES ONLY, bump across the lawn, and park crookedly in the space reserved for the deputy headmaster.

'That's her,' said Tracey, watching her get out of the car.

It had to be. Only someone called Miss Blackstone could be so gross, so ugly, so badly dressed, so utterly opposite from everything Miss Fabergé had stood for.

She was tall and heavily built. She wore flat, thick shoes like a man's, with ankle socks instead of stockings, and a checked skirt that looked like a horse blanket. She wore no make-up, and her hair, flattened to her head by the rain, was so thin that her white scalp shone through.

'She needs a hat with horns,' said Marianne. She giggled as the woman, covering her head with a newspaper, lumbered towards the verandah. 'And saucepan lids for her chest.'

'I think she needs a broomstick,' muttered Tracey.

They met officially a few minutes later when the bell went for assembly. The whole school, smelling of wet wool, squeezed into the hall to mumble its way through the oath of allegiance and the national anthem, and to salute the flag, which was hanging in a corner of the hall like damp washing.

Miss Blackstone stood on the stage with the rest of the staff, and stared down at them.

If Tracey had needed another reason to dislike Miss Blackstone, that stare was enough. There was something unnerving about it; even at this distance her eyes looked odd: they were pale and round, as if she had found them in a river-bed.

Tracey suppressed a giggle; she had a sudden image of Miss Blackstone fossicking among the pebbles in a dry river, trying them in her eye-sockets until she found a pair she liked.

She nudged Marianne, wanting to share the joke with her, and in that moment found herself looking straight into those terrible eyes. A fear as cold as stone struck through her; in panic she fixed her eyes on a portrait of the Queen that hung at the back of the stage, and pretended she had been looking at that all along.

Marianne nudged her in return. 'What?'

Tracey, still staring at the Queen in case she met Miss Blackstone's eye, struggled to remember. But the joke had withered and died.

'Go on,' said Marianne, nudging her again. 'What was it?' But try as she might, Tracey could not remember what she had wanted to say; her mind had gone quite blank.

And that was when she realised she had been mind-razed.

She had all the symptoms: a vague tingling in her hands and feet, a sudden absence of memory, and a lingering dislike of the pebbly-eyed person who had caused it.

Tracey had no doubt it was Miss Blackstone. She remembered those pale eyes; they were just the sort of eyes you would expect to find on someone who could raze minds.

It followed that Miss Blackstone was an alien. That also explained the terrible dress sense.

Up on the stage the headmaster announced a new bus timetable and cancelled the swimming, and then he introduced Miss Blackstone to the school and told everyone to 'welcome her by acclamation'.

He didn't tell them that she had the power to raze minds, thought Tracey; but that might be because he hadn't found out yet.

Tracey clapped along with everyone else, so as not to draw attention to herself. She clapped the way Miss Fabergé used to, elegantly patting her palm with her fingertips, and she was pleased to find how little noise it made.

She was also pleased to find that the mind-razing had not been entirely successful: she still remembered who Miss Fabergé was.

Tracey intended to keep her discovery to herself for a while; she had found that people did not always believe her when she told them extraordinary things. This time, she told herself, she would watch and wait and gather evidence, and not tell anyone until she had absolute proof.

But because Marianne was her friend, she let her into the secret while they walked along the verandah to their classroom.

'I don't believe you!' said Marianne. It was what she always said.

'Didn't you see her eyes?' said Tracey, 'They were like ... like ... I forget what they were like,' she said, puzzled.

'Last year,' said Marianne, 'you thought your neighbours were aliens. You said that two aliens disguised as an elderly couple had rented the house next door and were using it as a communications base.'

'You thought so too!' said Tracey.

'Only because you talked me into it.'

When they got to the classroom Miss Blackstone was already waiting for them. 'See what I mean?' whispered Tracey. 'How could she have got here so fast?'

Some crawler had written WELCOME MISS BLACKSTONE across the blackboard in red chalk. It would be a week before anyone could get it off, but nevertheless Miss Blackstone, after a jovial thank you, was making everybody try.

While they took it in turns to rub away at the board Miss Blackstone moved her table from the corner of the room to the middle, and sat on it.

'I'm your new class teacher,' she said. Since this was something they all knew, everyone started shuffling their feet and rattling pencil cases and looking for rubber bands to flick.

Miss Blackstone took no notice. 'I'm going to teach the same subjects that Miss Fabergé did,' – a sigh of regret went up from the class at the mention of Miss Fabergé's name – 'and I expect you all to work. There'll be homework. And there'll be tests.'

'Now do you believe me?' whispered Tracey.

And as Miss Blackstone settled herself more comfortably on the table, Tracey, with the miserable person's determination to find even more cause for misery, noticed something else: under her ankle socks she was wearing stockings.

She did not tell Marianne at once for fear of being mind-razed again, but at lunchtime when the rain had stopped and they were sitting under the pine trees, she made Marianne watch as Miss Blackstone marched across the yard.

'See that?' said Tracey, pointing at the stockings. 'What did I tell you?'

'That doesn't mean she's an alien,' said Marianne. 'She might just have cold legs.'

'Miss Fabergé used to wear boots,' said Tracey. 'Creamy-coloured suede ones, with little gold buckles.'

Just then Miss Blackstone saw them and waved. Tracey, mindful of the eyes, looked away and studied a line of black ants that was escaping to higher ground. But she knew without looking that Miss Blackstone was coming over to them. With a slow, deadly compulsion, as if she were locked on a tractor beam, Tracey found herself turning away from the black ants and looking up. Miss Blackstone had just joined them.

'I wonder if you would help me,' said Miss Blackstone, beaming at them. 'I have some things to put in the car.'

Tracey stared at the tip of Miss Blackstone's nose. Not only was it safer than looking at her eyes, it was more interesting: the cold had reddened it, giving her an unexpectedly jolly look, like Father Christmas.

'I'd be awfully grateful,' said Miss Blackstone.

Marianne, who was like putty in anyone's hands, fell for it. 'I'll help you,' she said, jumping up.

And Tracey, who could not let her best friend walk into danger alone, had to go with her. She cheered herself up by deciding it was a chance to gather clues.

But she was disappointed. There were no clues. Besides putting equipment in her car for sport that afternoon, Miss Blackstone was just removing some of the bits and pieces Miss Fabergé had left behind.

Although Miss Fabergé's outward appearance had always been perfect (even the wayward little curls that fluttered round her face had not really escaped, but had been put there by a hairdresser), her desk was a strange contradiction. Once when Miss Fabergé was rummaging through it looking for the class roll, Tracey looked over her shoulder and saw a surprising jumble of books, tissues, jars of cream, lipsticks, felt-pens, nail files and empty perfume bottles.

It had given Tracey a feeling of tenderness to know that Miss Fabergé wasn't perfect.

But now Miss Blackstone took from Miss Fabergé's desk the few things that were left – a half-used lipstick, an emery board, a knitting needle, a used-up note pad – and dropped them in a plastic bag. She sealed the top with sticky tape and tossed it on the back seat of the car.

Tracey felt a dark, mutinous rage bubble up within her.

'They do that in gaol,' said Marianne later on, as they were walking down to the sports oval. 'And with dead people.'

'Do what?' said Tracey.

'Put their things in a plastic bag,' said Marianne. 'That's what my uncle reckons.' Marianne's uncle was a policeman.

Tracey was struck by an idea that was perfect and breathtaking in its simplicity. Suddenly everything was clear, suddenly everything fitted: the mind-razing, the collecting of Miss Fabergé's things, everything.

'Miss Fabergé's been kidnapped,' she said.

Marianne stood still. 'Don't be stupid.'

'Miss Blackstone did it. First she mind-razed her, then she kidnapped her.'

'Whatever for?'

'How would I know? So that she could take her place, I suppose. That's what aliens do, isn't it? I expect Miss Fabergé's being held prisoner in Miss Blackstone's house – in a huge, dark mansion covered in creeper, with bars over the windows.'

'Miss Blackstone lives in the block of flats just down from the laundromat,' said Marianne. 'Eleven A. My uncle helped her move in.' Marianne's other uncle was a removalist.

The mention of Marianne's uncle – even the wrong one – made Tracey think of getting her to tell the right uncle – the policeman – about Miss Fabergé's predicament.

But then she realised it could be embarrassing. She had met him once before, when she had to explain to him why she was trespassing on next door's property with a yellow bucket on her head. The bucket had been to ward off death rays, and was very successful – she was still alive to be embarrassed – but Marianne's uncle, who must have been slightly affected by the rays, did not believe her.

'And that's the silliest thing I ever heard of,' said Marianne, after a pause in which she had apparently considered all the other silly things she had heard of.

'Are you going to help me?' asked Tracey.

'No.'

Tracey was silent. Clearly she would have to rescue Miss Fabergé herself.

She thought for a while about asking one of the boys to help her. It was always more interesting to do these things in company, and there were one or two boys whose company she quite liked. But there was the problem of getting them to

151

believe her; if she hadn't been able to convince Marianne, she didn't think she could convince anyone else.

She thought about it all through sport, and got her shins bruised as a result. But by half-past three she could see there was no alternative.

'I'll go by myself,' she told Marianne. 'Even though I'm not sure which flat it is, and even though I might get into trouble.'

'I'll show you which flat it is,' said Marianne. 'But from across the street. I'm not coming any closer, okay?'

The block of flats was disappointingly ordinary. None of the flats had bars over the windows; none of them had strange antennae on the roof; there was no hum of alien machinery coming from deep inside.

The building was ordinary pale-coloured brick, with ordinary prickly plants in a garden of pale, round river stones. The stones reminded Tracey of something; she stared at them for several seconds, trying to think what it was, but her mind was a blank.

The door of Number Eleven A was painted a sunny yellow that was beginning to peel, and the number was askew.

Before Tracey had time to knock, Miss Blackstone opened the door and beamed at her. 'Tracey!' she said. 'I was wondering when you'd get here. Come on in.'

Tracey clutched her school bag more tightly – her palms were beginning to sweat – fixed her eyes on the third button from the top of Miss Blackstone's shirt, and edged inside.

The inside of the flat was just as disappointingly ordinary as the outside. There was a beige self-patterned carpet, striped curtains, a table, some chairs, a sofa, and bookcases with books in them. Nothing else.

'I'm just having a cup of tea or coffee,' said Miss Blackstone. 'Would you like one?'

Tracey hesitated. There could be worse things than mind-razing; a cup of alien tea or coffee might be one of them.

Miss Blackstone went into the kitchen. 'I'll make you one anyway,' she called back.

While Miss Blackstone was out of the way Tracey examined what she could see of the flat. It was significant, she thought, that the flat was so tidy. There were no newspapers on the sofa, no Lotto forms on the table, no scissors or old light bills on the mantelpiece like there were at home. In particular there were no signs of Miss Fabergé such as lipsticks or empty perfume bottles; obviously Miss Blackstone had tidied them away.

That was where aliens slipped up, thought Tracey. They never could understand how sloppy human beings were.

But although the room showed no sign of human occupancy, it showed no sign of alien occupancy either. There were no tall cylinders made of perspex, and no strange-looking radios; there were no star maps on the wall, and no control consoles with flashing lights.

'I know what you're thinking,' said Miss Blackstone, coming back with two mugs and a packet of biscuits.

Tracey jumped.

'You're wondering whether it's tea or coffee,' said Miss Blackstone, putting the mugs on the table. 'I'm afraid I can't tell you. It tastes like a mixture of both; I got it from the school canteen.'

For the first time that day Tracey felt reassured. She had once tasted school tea or coffee at a film night, and knew that no alien would ever touch it. Aliens had their own food, which came in jewel colours of blue, green and purple, and they got it from dispensers built into the wall. There were no such dispensers here.

She helped herself to a mug of whatever it was, and was pleased to find it tasted exactly like the tea or coffee at school film nights.

'I got it because I knew you were coming,' said Miss Blackstone. 'Normally I wouldn't touch the stuff.'

Tracey choked into her mug, realising her mistake.

Just then a door to another room swung open and a blonde dishevelled figure wearing cream boots and a matching suede suit tottered out. 'Oh, goodness gracious,' it murmured. 'Just look at this skirt. I'll never get the creases out.'

'Miss Fabergé!' yelled Tracey.

Miss Fabergé turned to look at her. 'Tracey, isn't it? How sweet of you to come.' Miss Fabergé's eyes as she looked at Tracey seemed vague, almost dazed, and there was a smudge on her cheek that looked like grease. Tracey felt a pang of fear.

'Are you all right?' she whispered.

'Oh, I'm fine, fine, don't you worry about that,' said Miss Fabergé. 'Why don't you take a half day off?'

Tracey told her school was over for the day.

'Tomorrow, then,' said Miss Fabergé with her sweet smile, and started filing her nails. Miss Blackstone watched her.

Tracey watched both of them. She was thinking of all the films she had seen in which the hero said 'If I'm not back in ten minutes, call the cops,' and she wished she had said something of the sort to Marianne, with instructions of course to make sure it wasn't her uncle.

She glanced at the window to see if Marianne was still outside, but a lace curtain spoiled her view. And then she caught sight of something else: on the floor under the table there was an old-fashioned black telephone.

A telephone!

She edged towards it.

'Leave that alone.' Miss Blackstone's voice was jovial as ever, but her foot pushed the phone out of reach. Tracey moved back again. She was not particularly disappointed; she had not been looking forward to telling the operator that she was imprisoned in a flat by an alien.

She looked round, at the ordinary flat with its ordinary decoration, at Miss Blackstone quietly sipping her coffee or

154

tea, and Miss Fabergé noisily filing her nails. Miss Fabergé didn't seem to be in any danger; surely all Tracey had to do was simply stand up, announce she was going home, and go.

She half-closed her eyes and rehearsed it in her mind: she would get up and say 'Thank you for the tea or coffee,' and make straight for the door.

She opened her eyes and studied the door to see where the handle and catches were.

'Have I got the right earrings on?' asked Miss Fabergé, peering up at Miss Blackstone.

'They look fine to me,' said Miss Blackstone.

That decided it. The thought of leaving the elegant Miss Fabergé to the mercy of Miss Blackstone's fashion sense was more than Tracey could bear. She would take Miss Fabergé with her, no matter what the cost. She stood up. 'Come on, Miss Fabergé,' she said. 'We're leaving.'

'Oh, no,' said Miss Fabergé. 'I couldn't. I definitely have to stay here.'

'No, you don't,' said Tracey. 'You just think you have to because you've been mind-razed. But if you come with me we'll find a doctor or something. You'll be all right, honest.'

Miss Blackstone moved in front of the door. 'That's very kind of you, Tracey,' – she gave Tracey one of her beaming smiles – 'but Miss Fabergé hasn't been very well, and she really does have to stay here till she's better.'

The rage that had bubbled in Tracey earlier now overflowed. 'I know what you're up to!' she yelled. 'Don't think I don't know because I do! I know exactly what you're doing!'

Miss Blackstone looked surprised, then pleased. 'Really?'

Tracey nodded. 'Yes,' she said, but with a little less certainty this time.

'In that case,' said Miss Blackstone, looking rather relieved, 'you must know that this teaching android has been malfunctioning for some time. It's been giving us no end of trouble.'

'I'm fine, just a little malfunction, don't you worry about that,' said Miss Fabergé, dabbing lipstick on her fingernails.

'We've had several tries at getting it to self-repair,' said Miss Blackstone, 'but without any luck; and that's why I've been called in. Well,' she corrected herself, 'down, really.'

In answer to Tracey's look she explained, 'I'm an android mechanic.'

Slowly Tracey got up. She went over to the door that Miss Fabergé had tottered through, and pushed it open.

In the room were two large perspex cylinders, some strange-looking radios, a control console with flashing lights, and an illuminated star map. Set into one wall was a slot with a glass door in front, and beside it were pictures of jelly in jewel colours of blue, green and purple.

'There'll be homework when I'm better, you'll see, my word there will be,' said Miss Fabergé, dabbing lipstick on her ears.

Miss Blackstone kicked the black telephone further under the table. 'Don't use that telephone, it's a direct line to Vega – for ordering parts and so on. If you want an ordinary phone there's one in the kitchen.'

'You mean I'm allowed to ring up?' asked Tracey.

'Why not?' asked Miss Blackstone.

Tracey thought about that for a while. But since she could not think of anyone she fancied telling her story to, it did not help her very much.

'Am I allowed to go home?'

'If you like,' said Miss Blackstone.

'Well,' said Tracey, 'thank you for the tea or coffee, then.' She started towards the door.

'It was a pleasure,' said Miss Blackstone, opening it for her. 'You must come again some time.'

Tracey took one last look at Miss Fabergé, who was dabbing lipstick on her nose. 'Goodbye, Miss Fabergé.'

'Oh, not goodbye, *au revoir*,' said Miss Fabergé. 'A number,

n, increases as the square of its homework and earrings, and certain logical outputs vary indiscriminately.'

'Thank you,' whispered Tracey, and slipped out.

Marianne, who had been waiting in the laundromat, came to meet her. 'What on earth have you been doing? I've been freezing out here. I thought you were never coming out.'

Tracey was startled to find it was nearly dark; it gave her an odd, unreal feeling, as if she had just come out of a cinema. 'Well?' said Marianne. 'Did you rescue her?'

'No,' said Tracey.

'I told you it was a dumb idea,' said Marianne.

Miss Blackstone taught them for a week, and then on Monday morning, to everyone's delight, Miss Fabergé came back. She was as pretty and as elegant as ever, but something about her seemed to have changed. She set homework, for one thing; and she was strict about punctuality. And she arranged the few things in her desk – the roll, two books and a pen – with studied, meticulous care.

Miss Blackstone moved out of her flat at the end of the week, according to Marianne, whose uncle helped her move. And by a coincidence, Tracey's next-door neighbours, the elderly couple, moved on the same day. They left behind a lot of rubbish – perspex cylinders, strange-looking radios, consoles with flashing lights, and the like – which the next occupants, with a good deal of grumbling, carted to the tip.

SILENT REPORTER
Frank Willmott

MEMO:	MMMCXVII XV MCMLXXXVIII
TO:	Angel Benny [Observations]
ASSIGNMENT:	Proceed to Neighbourhood Zone 3999 Blue, Planet Earth. Report on new developments of the heart, 112/114 Caldwell Street.
FROM:	Angel Grace, FS&HG Prospects Division, HEAVEN

The house was an older-styled weatherboard one, its verandah almost concealed by a forest of trees. Benny reached out

and felt the coarseness of a fence-picket, the surface mois-
ture of an overhanging leaf, and grinned with contentment.
He glanced about. Two women came hurrying towards him,
their faces hidden beneath head-scarfs, their low chatter and
boot heels echoing along the patched bitumen street. In
driveways car exhausts spluttered white smoke; a cat licked
itself where it sat among the garbage spill outside the next-
door flats, its marmalade fur caught in a creeping shadow of
early morning light. It still felt the same after fifteen years.

He found the family seated at the breakfast table, the father
pulling faces at his small daughter who exposed a mouthful
of toast and jam as she chewed. The man was dressed in
overalls, had restless eyes that kept returning to the yard of
fruit trees, vines, and vegetable mounds outside.

'Yum yum, bubble-gum!' cackled the boy as he perched on
the edge of his chair, trying to impress his older sister, 'Stick
your finger up your ...'

'That's enough, I said!' the mother said tersely. 'And sit up
properly or get down. I'd just like to finish a conversation
with your father for once.'

The boy jutted his bottom lip out like a clowning chimpan-
zee, then jumped down on the rug and began to construct a
space station from his scattered Mobilo. There was enough
food lying beneath his chair and the table, mused Benny, to
feed one of Heaven's alleycats for a week. He slipped down
beside the boy and studied his quiet intelligence as he
became absorbed in linking the pieces. He was proving to his
sister that he could also be clever. His thoughts were tied to
her presence. Jess made up most of Louie's world. Benny
glanced up at her. She was half involved in listening to her
parents' conversation while using her colours to make a
card for her nanny. She loved making cards for people, and
imagined they loved her for doing it.

160

'Well! What are we going to do? The money for the car rego!' the woman frowned. Her legs were never still beneath the table. 'Doesn't it concern you just a little, Mike?'

His eyes diverted from a partially-built cubby on poles at the bottom of the yard to the row of flats over the side paling fence.

'You know what?' he said.

'What?'

'What I'd like to do!'

'What's that?'

'Pull down the side fence.'

Benny moved closer and in Mike's head saw a neighbourhood where there were no dividing fences; instead houses and flats linked by a network of shared vegetable patches, greenhouses, pottery sheds, workshops, chicken pens, treehouses, adventure playgrounds.

'One fence, Mike,' Linda stared at him. 'And I just wonder about it, anyway.'

The cubby's poles had been sunk against an olive tree. Benny was studying its potential for doubling as a treehouse when there was a bang on the side fence, and a head appeared.

'Hi!' called a boy with a plump face and squeaky voice. 'Working on the cubby for the little girl and boy? Can I help?'

Mike straightened, and wiping sawdust down his sides, stared despairingly at Jess and Louie running about with his tools.

'Don't know how you can help, Salvo,' he muttered.

The head disappeared and within moments the boy came puffing into the yard.

'Anything!' he said, picking up a hammer. 'I can use this. What nails will I hit?'

'I'm not doing ...'

'What's this?' asked the boy, examining the spirit level. And then two more heads had appeared at the fence, talking quietly as they stared up at the cubby construction.

'Very good,' said one of the men, thrusting his cigarettes towards Mike. His combed-back hair glistened; the smile was a little forced. Salvo fell quiet on seeing his father there. Beside him stared the pinched grinning eyes of an old man who wore a tarboosh and a woollen scarf across his mouth. He was a neighbour from the flats. Benny watched Mike wave the cigarettes away politely and, clearing a leg from the loops of power cord, return to sawing lengths of wood with an intense expression.

'How old are you?' Jess asked Salvo as she swung from a bough.

'Twelve.'

'I'm nearly seven. I'm in Grade One,' she panted. 'Louie's only four. Sarah, my cousin, is eleven and Paul is old and Julie at school . . .'

But Salvo wasn't listening. His eyes were fixed on the cubby taking shape above. Benny felt the envy, searched the images in the boy's mind for an understanding. Among them was a small bedroom shared with a baby sister and a violent-tempered elder brother who pounded its walls as if in a cage.

'It's going to be beautiful, this cubby,' Salvo said, as the scream of the power-saw subsided. 'I was thinking . . . I wish I had some nails. Can I borrow a hammer, Mike? I wanna build a billycart. You don't have any wheels do ya? You know, just what you don't want!'

On the Monday morning Benny went with Salvo to school. He wandered about the classroom, tuning in and out of the busy world of daydreams, his head filled with his own memories. Three years, that's all he had had at high school. Death didn't hurt when it was so sudden and unexpected; it simply left an empty seat; a gap in the world to be filled. The angel sat beside Salvo whose keen face didn't betray the voice inside screaming out for the teacher to slow down. There was frustration there, always trying to keep in touch; and fear of already having lost the race. Salvo's thoughts began to branch like the limbs of a tree. He was pumping weights and shedding fat; standing up to Tony, his older brother, telling him to think of other people too; telling his dad that any job was better than an invalid's pension; telling his mum didn't she know Tina, his little sister, was always asleep when she got home from work at night; telling them they shouldn't keep shifting because their homes kept getting smaller and there was no room for a bike. And then the angel saw the boy's features relax. The cubby had risen up in his thoughts. It was his cubby. His home.

Benny found them dawdling between bicycle shops on the way home. Salvo had a love affair with bikes; collecting parts. With his face pressed against one shop-window he cursed his mother for not letting him have one. Just a few scratches on a refrigerator. Some torn fly-wire. Where else was he supposed to keep it? Again the angel was filled with memories. He sighed and, turning to face the noise of the traffic, suddenly recalled that the factory where his mother once worked was just around the corner. He was there in seconds, standing before the large tin door where he had waited so often for his mother to spill out with the other Italian women. Inside the place looked the same; rows of sewing-machines; piles of shirts; fabric cones and stacks; except now the faces belonged to young Vietnamese women. On the spur of the moment he rose up and flew to another part of the neighbourhood, and descended onto the pavement before a small cottage among the squash of houses. It had changed, the brick-cladding gone, his old bedroom now part of a sunroom. His family was also long gone;

his little sister even had two children of her own. He was never out of touch, received all the messages from his mother. She kept his memory safe in their thoughts.

Salvo cursed himself for having lost his key; cursed his father for not letting him have another one. He began to hammer on the door again until the edge of his fist grew tender. The flat's darkness meant nothing. Tony could sleep through an earthquake. Why weren't his father and little sister home yet? It was growing dark: the streetlights were on. It was freezing cold. He hammered some more and then sat down on the step and hugged his body. He wanted to cry, to be a baby, when suddenly he felt calm, as if good thoughts had been placed inside his head. At his back the door of the flat eased softly open.

'What! What!' he kept repeating as he entered the empty flat, his large eyes tentatively looking behind the door. 'How? Like magic! It opened!'

Mike held a weatherboard in position and hammered the nails in. Benny watched him reach for the next, seeing inside the man the little boy excitedly rushing to finish his cubby he had always wanted.

'Beautiful!' Salvo's voice croaked. He stood on the middle step with his head poked inside. 'Our cubby is going to be the best in the world. I didn't mean ours. Youse two,' he said to Jess and Louie. 'Youse two are the luckiest children in the world. When I grow up, Mike, I'm going to be a dad just like you . . . making things for my children.'

Benny watched the hammer pause in Mike's hand; felt the rush of guilt engulf him. But the angel turned when he felt another source of emotion, far stronger, although further away. In a knot-hole in one of the palings of the side fence he saw an eye flinch. Salvo's father hid there, and he paused to stare down at his nicotined fingers crippled by arthritis.

'Mike! Can I ask you a favour?' Salvo was saying. 'Would you buy me a bike? I'd give you the money. And could I keep it in your place?'

'Ah, hello, Mike!' Salvo's father called sheepishly, his head surfacing at the fence. 'Very good.' He stared at his son and his face hardened. 'Salvo!' he said threateningly. 'Come home now.'

Benny awoke to the sound of voices out in the street, drunken voices, echoing like the howl of wolves.

'Come out, wog!' they screamed. 'We know you're in there! The money, Tony! You're gonna get yours, wop!'

The angel glanced at Louie who was deep in dreams about battling transformer robots, and then turned to where Jess slept. Behind her small abandoned features she was also lost in a dream, tucked up in bed against her nanny's soft chest and the sweet smell of her nightie.

'I always pray,' her nanny was saying softly.

'Nanny! Mummy and Daddy said they don't believe in God.'

'Then it'll be our little secret,' the elderly woman smiled.

In an instant the angel remembered the other small girl close by and reaching through walls and a paling fence he placed his fingertips on Tina's eyelids to deepen her sleep and protect her against the world of waking.

The sharp leaves prickled his wings as Benny sat in the olive tree, listening to Louie's story. With legs crossed the boy sat in the cubby, methodically turning the pages of a picture book as he read by memory the story of 'Goorialla, the Rainbow Serpent' to a wide-eyed Salvo. Salvo was spellbound by the vivid colours of the pictures, by Louie's ability to read.

'What are youse doing?' Jess said, suddenly leaping up the ladder.

'No!' screamed Louie. 'You can't come in!'

'Course I can!'

'No! No girls allowed.'

'That's right,' Salvo said, looking about.

'Who said?'

'Daddy!' Louie replied, jutting out his jaw.

'Liar, liar, pants on fire!' Jess said, incensed; and lunging, she took a swipe at the book.

Louie dropped it, and doing his monkey squeal, flung open the secret exit door, catching the surprised angel a stinging blow across the shins.

They were all settling down for a meal in front of the fire when the front doorbell rang. Mike exchanged a knowing glance with Linda, then hauling himself up wearily, went to answer it.

'Salvo?' she said, when he returned.

'He said his dad wants to see me.'

Anger flared in his wife's eyes.

'Tell him you're just about to start tea.'

Mike shrugged and pulled a face.

'I won't be a minute,' he said. He turned to leave.

'I'm going too!' said Jess, jumping after him. Benny followed them to Salvo's place where they found his father slumped forward on the couch, flicking ash into a cupped hand as he watched a video.

'Please, Mike, sit,' he said, looking up. He waved a hand at the screen. 'A Little Tony movie. You know it?' He muttered something to Salvo.

'My dad don't speak good English,' Salvo said, looking uncomfortable. 'He says, "You want some wine?"'

'No thanks. I'm about to have tea.'

Salvo spoke to his father who waved him away to get the wine anyway. Benny watched Tina, the little girl, jumping around the small table that dominated the room, wiping it over and over again with a dripping kitchen sponge. She was pretending to be a mother, and they were all her children.

'Tell my dad I can have a bike,' said Salvo returning.

'Ah, Mike,' his father frowned. 'No bike here. Traffic is very bad.'

The father's comment opened up a large empty pit inside the angel's stomach. He felt sudden painless death once more.

'I love bikes.'

The father spoke once more to Salvo, and the boy began to protest.

'My dad . . .' he said sheepishly. 'My dad wants you to . . . I'll show you.' He picked up a school folder and opened it before Mike. 'You see my dad's not smart and I have my homework and I can't read the words . . .'

'Can I help, Mike?' asked Salvo, bustling into the yard. It wasn't the right time. Benny had observed the fuses in Mike's head burn out one by one during a day of frustrations.

'No,' he answered grimly, struggling to push the blade of his spade into soil baked hard by the past summer.

'What are you doin', Mike?'

'Starting to put the vegetable plots to bed.'

'I'll just watch.'

'No.'

'I won't get in ya way.'

'I'd prefer if you went home.'

He watched Salvo mooch off down the side, and went on digging until suddenly becoming aware of a head at the fence.

'I'm on this side,' Salvo said. He stayed there for a while, watching with puppy-dog eyes, then disappeared for fifteen minutes, only to reappear with his father and the old neighbour.

'Have you got another spade my dad can borrow?' called Salvo. 'And one of those pick things?'

Mike found the tools and passed them over the fence without offering a greeting. He worked on, a cloud hanging over his thoughts until finally he couldn't resist, and took a peek through the fence. The two men had nearly finished turning over a small square of lawn at the end of the flats' driveway. They were taking a breather, having a smoke as they both grinned down at the neatly turned earth. With a smile and a shake of the head Mike returned to his job. Moments later there was a kick at the fence, and Salvo appeared.

'My dad wants to know if you've got any flowers.'

'Flowers?' Mike frowned.

'Not flowers . . . you know! The seed things!'

'No.'

'What's that?' Salvo said, staring at the woodpile beside the shed.

'Wood for the fires inside. You can't grow it.'

Salvo disappeared for another ten minutes.

'Can I ask you something, Mike?' he said, there once more, his eyes thinking aloud. 'Would it be all right to light a fire on the concrete in the driveway?'

'I don't know.'

'My dad and the neighbour man like to sit by a fire and talk.'

Mike sighed and, peering around at the dull light, began to gather up the tools.

'The only problem is we don't have any wood to burn.' Salvo's begging tone followed him into the shed.

Benny stared down at the fresh glistening colours in the tossed salad. Even they didn't lift the mood in the kitchen.

'The firewood!' Linda said through clenched teeth. 'Bloody hell, they've got a nerve. What did you say to them?'

Mike stared at the table with a glazed expression.

'I didn't say anything,' he mumbled.

'So do you still want to tear the fence down?'

Benny watched him closely but he still didn't have anything to say, and for a moment even his thoughts were undefined.

'Do you know what she's been doing for the last hour?' Linda said, pointing through to where Jess was at the table, making another card. 'This one's for Salvo's father. She said she feels sorry for him. It's all a bit much.'

The angel rose up. He had to be elsewhere, alone, to think about his report. Time had almost run out. He flew east a few blocks to an intersection between two narrow main roads and paused by the curb. A patch of freckled concrete with an irregular join sparkled beneath the street lights; the join causing car tyres to thud as they skimmed over it. It was the spot where his life had ended, one week before his fifteenth birthday. Now his memory belonged as much to another lifetime. Why had they chosen his old neighbourhood for an assignment? And why was he compelled to return to this intersection now? Hadn't all demons been put to rest? Benny stayed for some time at that very spot until he understood.

Once more he rose up and, following the railway line, swooped south, leaving behind the townhall clock, the baths' floodlit blue rectangle, the old stockyards and bluestone warehouses, and the graffitied message on a lonely alleyway wall: ALL LIFEFORM ON EARTH IS DEAD: BEAM ME UP, SCOTTY. He passed by the city lights and the river, and continued south where the houses were so grand, and where the air of wealth and indifference chilled his wings. Gradually darkness set in below, and at once the stars became his light.

On a small countryside property a man held back the lounge room curtain and stared briefly out at the night. Down by the track, where the gums rustled against the night wind, he gazed at the giant woodstacks that had remained there for fifteen years: monuments to his crime, the day his truck had crushed a bicycle and young boy's life for the sake of a red light. The truck was gone; anxiety had stolen his mid-life. As he stood and stared, a strange feeling overcame him; a feeling he hadn't known for so long. He suddenly saw the beauty of the night; the beauty of being alive; of a time to accept. It felt as though hands were on his shoulders; hands as light and gentle as these new thoughts.

Mike waited for Jess to fetch her card and they wandered around to the flat. They knocked on Salvo's door but no one answered.

'You know where they are?' called a voice. The owner of the flats came hurrying from around the back.

'Not here?' asked Mike.

'No,' spat the owner. 'They leave in the middle of the night. Bloody bastards. Bloody pigs. Two months rent they owe.' He pointed a finger up the driveway. Sweat glistened above his lip. 'They dig up the lawn, see! Make a fire on the driveway. Leave it filthy. Bloody bastards.'

Beyond the owner's bald head Mike saw the curtain of one flat slightly pulled and the old Egyptian's eyes peering out. He took Jess's hand and started to return home.

'Why you no cut your trees?' called the owner behind them. 'See the mess of leaves on the ground.'

They stood at their front gate, Jess watching her father closely. His eyes were squeezed against the low morning sun.

'What, Daddy?' she asked.

'I was just wondering.'

'What?'

'How come we've been living here for six years and don't know our neighbours?'

'Salvo's not a pig, Daddy.'

'No.' Her father smiled down at her. 'You know what we should do?'

'What?'

'Organise one of those street parties.'

'Yeahhhh!' her eyes widened.

'And you can do the invitations.'

'Okay!'

As they turned to go inside for breakfast a gentle breath-like breeze blew the card from her grasp. Jess turned to see an angel pick it up and put it in his pocket.

'Beam me up, Grace,' she thought she heard him say.

MEMO:	MMMCXIX
TO:	Angel Grace [Prospects]
COMMENTS:	Dreams remain at location, everywhere; while humans remain imperfect. Request transfer to Guardians' Division, and assignment to Earth where business remains incomplete.
FROM:	Angel Benny.

THE MIMICS
Thurley Fowler

Joey heard the approaching car and began tossing tennis balls into the plastic bucket. A few were fluffy yellow, but most were well worn, with some khaki, almost bald and bounceless. Those nearby were in first, and then he grabbed the bucket by the handle and sprinted to collect the strays.

The car was getting closer and the trail of dust behind it was red and angry.

In his haste he fumbled, jolting the bucket so that it spat balls at his feet.

'Stupid ... you rotten, stupid balls.' Somehow they were back in the bucket and he glanced with despair at a few yellow blobs on the far side of the court.

The car had squealed to a stop. The door burst open and a voice scorched the surface of the tennis courts.

'I've told you before! Get off these courts! At once! If I get my hands on you ...'

For a moment, Joey could not move, then, like the flock of galahs that had been feeding on the yellow grasses alongside the court, he fled.

The galahs wheeled away to nearby trees; he sped for the hole in the high wire-netting fence.

The lock on the gate was rattling as an irate man grappled with a key.

'You're all the same. Trouble, that's what you are – trouble.' Foxes or rabbits or kids had made that hole, and Joey had widened it for easy access. He and his bucket of balls and his racquet were through it, and his skinny dark legs could have out-sprinted any tennis official as he headed into the trees.

Soon he slowed to a jog, then stopped to observe a caterpillar, his brown eyes sparkling, his wide mouth smiling as it struggled from its outgrown skin.

'I soon lost him,' he told it, 'Silly old twit couldn't run the length of the court, anyway.'

He wiggled his toes in the early morning warmth of the red dust.

'Sorry, I can't help you, caterpillar, you seem to be stuck awful tight, but you've got to do it all by yourself. Just like me and my homework. That's what Miss Mackay says.'

'Now, let's see if the trapdoor spider's home,' he said as he moved to the shadows of a friendly she-oak. The small trapdoor was closed and he eased it open with a stick. 'Don't get nervous, spider, I won't hurt you. I can see your eyes when I look down your hole. Good morning, spider.'

An agitated spider appeared, groped for its door, then scurried back down its hole, blocking the entrance after it.

'That's it! Be like everyone else this morning. Grumpy and mean and rotten.'

Regretfully, Joey turned away. It was a school day, and he

supposed he had better go. He didn't like disappointing Miss Mackay.

The track wound through trees. As a tiny kid he had lived with his family and some others of their Aboriginal band in humpies nearby. It was hard to remember details, but he could recall the hessian walls and bits of corrugated iron and flattened kerosene tins somehow shielding them from most of the rain and wind.

He could remember collecting sticks for his mother so that she could cook their dinner on an open fire. The aroma of it all was with him still, and he could almost smell the tang of the fire, the finger-licking goodness of the contents of the black pot, and the stench of the dogs that pushed their way in for scraps.

And he could remember when the people of the town had built new houses for them ...

Ahead, he could hear raised voices and he began to run, his feet moving easily, his stomach, empty of breakfast and full of apprehension, rumbling.

He had seen the farmer before, and, as usual, the farmer was shouting.

'Look, Bert! Look at the time! You're supposed to be at my place sewing rice bags by now, but you're not, are you? You're here, doing nothing, and you're holding up the works, mate.'

His dad was acting like a guilty small boy, head down, scraping in the dust with the toe of his runner. Peering around the door were Joey's mother and grandmother, and clinging to their skirts were his two little sisters.

'You're the best I've ever had at sewing bags, Bert, but you're not much use to me here, are you?' The farmer was trying to be reasonable, and keep his temper, but you had the feeling he was about to crack. 'If this happens again, Bert, you're out.'

Joey's dad mumbled something and rubbed a stubbly chin with long, dark fingers, his forehead wrinkling, his eyes downcast still. His dad was great at mimicking people, especially white people like teachers and social workers and policemen and farmers. But not while they were watching.

'C'mon, Bert, toss your bike on the back of the ute. We're off, mate, like the milk that's been left out in the sun ... off.'

The sighs of his dad and the squeaks of his dad's bike were twin laments, and Joey shook his head as he watched the dusty departure.

Inside the kitchen, Joey's mum was giggling and his grandmother was pouring out cups of coffee.

'Where've you been, Joey?' Shaking with mirth, his mum slopped her coffee on the table. Hastily, Joey snatched for the homework book he had left there, but already it was smeared with butter. He groaned as he wiped it on his pants.

'Playing tennis. Why didn't dad go to work, anyway?'

'He thought he'd try for fish in the canal. He and your uncles. I told him he wouldn't get away with it.' Her coffee cup rattled, her tummy shook.

Joey went in search of his schoolbag and angrily thrust in the book he should have put in earlier. He straightened, then began sorting through clothes for a clean shirt. There weren't any. He inspected collars and chose the shirt with the cleanest, well, least dirty.

His mum and sisters were watching television in the lounge room, and back in the kitchen, his grandmother was dreamily sipping coffee.

People were often mad at his mum when she giggled like this and he had heard them make comments about stupidity, but even when you are only eleven, you can figure out adults. Especially with a very understanding teacher at school who spent a lot of time having long chats with you, discussing your problems.

'I'm hungry,' he told his grandmother, rattling a box of

breakfast cereal, 'and someone had better go to town today to shop or I'll really starve and we'll all be out catching rabbits for our tea.'

He poured the last of the milk into his bowl, then glanced at his grandmother. She had a way of looking out over your head, and you knew only her body was with you. Like the caterpillar that shed its skin and toddled away along a branch, grandmother zoomed away in spirit and left her wrinkled body behind.

'You're not with me, are you, Gran?' No, she wasn't with him. She would be back with her tribe, maybe as a young girl.

When the townspeople had built houses for them, Gran had hated it. He could still remember how she had caught a goanna, built a fire in the backyard and cooked the goanna as it had been cooked by Aboriginals down the centuries. His mum and dad had been mad at her and covered up the ashes as though some crime had been committed. The goanna had tasted great.

But Gran was sweet and gentle and had cuddled him and told him stories about the Dreamtime. As a little kid, he had hidden his face in her lap, fascinated by her tales of spirit beings. He had trembled at the 'Wadi Judjara' that could change shape and become goannas as well as people.

At first he had been scared of the spirit beings, but gradually they gave everything a deeper meaning. The smudge of the hills, the whisper of trees, the quiet starlit nights meant more when you knew that the spirit beings that had made them were out there still. Or had they? Were they? And did you believe it?

Angrily, he sprang to his feet, thumping the table so that everything on it jumped, his nostrils flaring.

'Where's my lunch? Did anyone get my lunch ready? I have to go to school NOW and I want my lunch.'

There was a scurry of feet and they were all looking at him with bewildered brown eyes, their hair tousled and curly, their lips full and red. His grandmother, still on her chair, her hands folded in her lap, his mother standing at the door of the kitchen, and his little sisters peeping around her skirt.

'I'm sorry, Joey,' his mother said. 'I was going to the shops yesterday, but I'll go today, instead. Take some money from the jar.'

'And my shirts are all dirty. Can you do some washing, please, Mum?'

She was nodding glibly, ready to promise anything. She found it hard to cope, Miss Mackay had said, and that was why she giggled and looked helpless. As a little girl, she had been taught to use a digging stick for witchetty grubs and little burrowing animals and to collect seeds and nuts and honey ants. Now, she had to shop at a supermarket.

He collected his schoolbag, and walked from the house, huffy still, not looking back at them or the house as he began to run.

He remembered moving into that house, with all the white people helping them and making such a fuss. Their band had lived in the Western Desert for many years and had spent some time in a reservation, before moving on to make their humpies on the outskirts of this town.

The only utensils Grandmother had used were those carved from wood, and then only for carrying water because her tribe did not heat water or boil food. She had laughed and laughed at the set of saucepans someone gave her.

'Welcome to your new home,' the white people had said, beaming their pleasure, and the noise of their departing cars could not drown their self-congratulation.

They made different sounds on their next visit, and were almost silent with horror on subsequent occasions.

Dad had stored wood in the bath, to keep it dry in the wet weather. He had hacked up some of the boards from the verandah for burning in the open fireplace. Much easier to do that than collect wood in the rain. Mum had ruined the electric stove in the first week, and after that had been much happier cooking their meals in the fireplace. Grandmother had burnt out all her saucepans.

The dogs slept on the beds and nobody had thought to demonstrate the art of mopping floors and cleaning sinks and stoves.

'We understand,' the white people had said, not understanding. 'We'll send social workers to help you, to show you what to do.'

The social workers came, but Grandmother would sit in a corner, look into space and not be with them in spirit. His mum and dad were like two naughty schoolkids, nodding heads and imitating actions. When the social workers went home, Dad would start his miming fun and Mum and Gran would fold up laughing, while the dogs crept back to the beds, and the clothes the social worker had washed flapped on the line.

Joey ran past the tennis court and along the main road to school.

'Here's trouble,' he muttered as he noted the empty playgrounds. 'Just as well Miss Mackay is my teacher. She understands.'

Miss Mackay was wonderful. She should have been cranky and bad-tempered, because she was tall and thin, with pulled-back grey hair and more sharp angles than a geometry lesson. Instead, she was sweet and soft-voiced and would listen seriously to the most outlandish excuse. Not that she would accept it without a shake of her head and twinkling eyes that let you know just what she thought of your efforts.

Confidently, he burst into the classroom. He dropped his schoolbag. His empty desk was an ocean away.

'And where have you been?'

It wasn't Miss Mackay. It was Mr Gill. He must be in the wrong class. No, he wasn't. There was Sam in the front seat and John Grey and Sarah Martin and ...

'I said ... Where have you been? And look at you ... Your shirt is ...' But the young Mr Gill choked on a description of Joey's shirt. His face reddened.

'Where is your homework, Joseph?'

His homework. In a moment he had the book from his bag and Mr Gill shuddered visibly at the sight of it. Joey looked hard at it himself, noting the dog-eared corners and the way the golf-ball sized smudge of butter had grown into bowling-ball size.

'Go to your desk, Joseph. You can stay in at lunch and re-write your homework in a new book. This one ...' Mr Gill held the book in two fingers and carried it to the waste paper basket which swallowed it, 'this one is not fit for any classroom.'

Of course, everyone had to laugh.

'Where's Miss Mackay?' Joey whispered to those around him, as he wriggled into his desk.

'Sick,' came back several answers.

'Quiet,' warned Mr Gill. 'Get to work, Joseph. At once.'

Joey searched noisily for a pen. His homework book. His good homework book, where he had spent hours wrestling with words and numbers and where Miss Mackay had gone over work so carefully with him until he understood. There was even a 'Very Good, Joey' and 'Improving, Joey' and once a star, a real gold star for excellent work, Miss Mackay had said. And Mr Gill had tossed it out. In the garbage bin. The garbage bin!

Things did not improve as the day progressed. His lunch-hour was lost. Jaded and tired and restless, he waited for the last session to pass.

'And now,' Mr Gill said, 'we'll study the first people who lived in Australia, The Aboriginals.'

There were giggles and someone poked Joey in the back. This is all I need, thought Joey. How did old Gill manage to think of it?

'Please, sir,' one of the boys asked, 'Joey's teeth always look whiter than ours. Are they? Or is it just because his face is black?'

There were shouts of laughter from the class and objections from Mr Gill. Joey sank deeper into the seat.

Mr Gill droned on, pausing for questions. The children, with the exception of one, were sitting forward, interested and alert. Mr Gill wrote headings on the board and a lively discussion followed each one.

'BELIEFS' scrawled the teacher.

'Now, one of the religious beliefs of the Aboriginals is the Dreamtime. They think that the earth and everything around us was made by spirit beings ... by strange creatures ... and these beings didn't die, but merged into the mountains and the rivers and rocks ... They think they're still out there, alive, living on in the Dreaming.'

There was astonishment and mirth.

'What do you think, Joey?' a boy called. 'D'you think there's bunyips in the bikeshed?'

'And elephants up the electric light poles?'

They were shouting with laughter, and Joey was huddled in shame. The sound of the bell released him, but everyone else seemed to leave the room with regret because they had been enjoying themselves so much.

He ran home, not noticing the court or checking on the trapdoor spider or any other creature. He could hear his dad on the front verandah, and he knew by the laughter that another mimicry session was in progress. Dad would be sewing imaginary rice bags, and the Boss and others would be impersonated. The laughter was loud and merry.

On the kitchen table was a bag of groceries. The butter was melting and a fly was sitting on the loaf of bread.

He ran into his room, grabbing his racquet and his bucket of old tennis balls. He had been planning it all the way home. What was the use of trying to be good at school and of staying out of trouble. He would go to the tennis court, but not to play tennis.

Of course, he would need his racquet as an alibi if caught. Out of his room, he flitted about the house, wanting something . . . something that was sharp and would dig . . .

The tomahawk.

He was on his way. Back through the trees, along the track, unseeing, his stomach tight, his whole being tense with fury. He was at the tennis court, scrambling on his knees through the hole.

He had always been a good boy. Never been naughty. Always behaved himself and tried to do his best. Until today.

If he couldn't play on the court, no one would. He would dig and dig and dig . . . Maybe his ancestors had dug with a digging stick for food; he was going to dig because he was angry, so angry that he wanted to be like that spider and shut himself away from everyone.

He dropped his racquet and placed the bucket near the exit, blindly clutching the tomahawk and running to the centre of the court.

'That you, Joey?' a voice called.

It was Sarah. Sarah Martin. She was at the gate on her bike.

He turned and raced for his bucket and racquet, knocking over things and fumbling and almost weeping in his haste. But she was there at the hole before him, hopping off her bike and leaning it against the fence.

'You play tennis, Joey?'

'Yes. When no one's around.' He stood up, hiding the tomahawk behind his back and she scrambled through the hole, picking up his racquet.

'I've never seen you here.'

'No. But I've seen you play.'

'You have?'

'Yes, I climb that big tree over there and watch on Saturdays.'

She made a few backhand practice swishes at an imaginary ball.

'Sorry all the kids laughed so much at your Dreamtime, Joey. They were stupid.' She was slim and fair and there were traces of green paint on her hair. His ancestors had smeared their bodies with mud to smother the human smell when hunting; his friends at school sometimes painted themselves for fun.

'After all, Joey, how we think everything began is a lot the same. They say there was The Big Bang, but my dad says that God must have planned it because, well, nothing was muddled up, was it?'

Joey shook his head. She was the best at debating in the class and had never lost an argument yet. Her eyes were big and blue and earnest.

'Now, if things had just happened, there would have been a mess, but everything was worked out ... like a million miracles, my dad says. Just look at a lizard's tiny little toes and the way a dandelion spreads its seeds ...'

Joey nodded mutely. She was the smartest person in school and talking in class was her only, but recurring, source of trouble.

'So we're like you, Joey. We believe a Great Spirit made everything and is out there alive still. So what's the difference?'

He grinned at her and she grinned back, handing him his racquet.

'So why do you only watch? Why don't you come and play?'

'They would chase me away. They always do.'

'No, they wouldn't, silly, not if you joined the club. Why don't you?'

'Me? I couldn't.' He swallowed.

'Why couldn't you? It doesn't cost much. Of course, you couldn't come along dressed like that ...'

Dress ... dress ... They were always worrying about the stupid clothes you wore!

'Could you buy white pants and shirt and tennis runners, d'you think? Get them for next Saturday and when I go home, I'll ask Dad how much it is to join and I'll tell you at school tomorrow.'

He had stopped breathing.

'Then, next Saturday morning at nine o'clock, you be here, and I'll take you to the coach. Could you do that?'

He was nodding. He could do that. He was sure he could.

'Now, two of the girls are meeting me here to play, so if you wanted to ...'

But, no, he was retreating already, with racquet and bucket and tomahawk. When he had his white clothes, he would play ... oh, how he would play ... how he would practise ... but not yet ... Not until Saturday.

He was through the hole, turning to shout his thanks, then running, running, running, wanting to throw up his arms and yell for joy, to hit the old tennis balls over the trees. Instead, he sobbed for breath, dark face screwed up in ecstasy.

And the spider heard him coming and hurriedly closed his trapdoor.